Benjamin Ellis Martin

In the Footprints of Charles Lamb

Benjamin Ellis Martin

In the Footprints of Charles Lamb

ISBN/EAN: 9783337251703

Printed in Europe, USA, Canada, Australia, Japan

Cover: Foto ©Andreas Hilbeck / pixelio.de

More available books at **www.hansebooks.com**

IN THE FOOTPRINTS OF
CHARLES LAMB

BY

Benjamin Ellis Martin

AUTHOR OF "OLD CHELSEA," ETC.

ILLUSTRATED BY HERBERT RAILTON
AND JOHN FULLEYLOVE

WITH A BIBLIOGRAPHY BY E. D. NORTH

NEW YORK
CHARLES SCRIBNER'S SONS
1894

Press of J. J. Little & Co.
Astor Place, New York.

TO
L. H. F.

DURING the half-century since the death of Charles Lamb, an immense mass of matter has been gathered about him and about his writings. In burrowing among the treasures and the rubbish of this mound, I have been struck by the total absence of what may be called a topographical biography of the man, or of any accurate record of his rovings : with the exception of that necessarily brief one contained in Mr. Laurence Hutton's invaluable " Literary Landmarks of London." Such a shortcoming is the more marked, inasmuch as Lamb is so closely identified with the Town. Not one among the men of letters, whose shadows walk the London streets with us, knew them better, or loved them more, than he did. In following his footsteps, I have found still untouched many of the houses that harboured him : and I have taken delight in the task, before the restless hand of reconstruction shall have plucked them forever away, of helping to keep alive the look of all that is left of the walls within which he lived and laboured.

From this mere memento of brick-and-mortar—all my original intent—I have been led on to a study of the man himself, from our more modern and more humane point of view. The time has long gone by for that kindly compact of reticence which may have been becoming in the years directly after his death. Nothing need be hidden now about the madness of Mary, about the terrible taking-off of her mother, about the early insanity of Charles himself, or his later weaknesses. And, in telling the entire truth, I have found comfort and cheer in the belief that neither apology nor homily can ever again be deemed needful to a decorous demeanour beside these dead.

So that I have sketched him just as he lives for me— the lines and the wrinkles of his aspect, the shine and the shadow of his soul : just as he moved in the crowd, among his friends, by his sister's side, and alone. To show exactly what he was, rather than what he did, I have used his own words wherever this was possible ; altering them as to their letter alone, where it has seemed essential. In this spirit of affectionate allegiance I have followed him faithfully in all his wanderings, from his cradle close by the Thames to his grave not far from the Lea.

B. E. M.

NEW YORK, October, 1890.

List of Illustrations.

List of Illustrations.

In the Footprints of Charles Lamb.

"The sun set ; but set not his hope :
Stars rose ; his faith was earlier up :
Fixed on the enormous galaxy,
Deeper and older seemed his eye :
And matched his sufferance sublime
The taciturnity of time.
He spoke, and words more soft than rain
Brought the Age of Gold again :
His action won such reverence sweet,
As hid all measure of the feat."

—EMERSON.

"Far from me, and from my friends, be such
frigid philosophy as may conduct us, indifferent
and unmoved, over any ground, which has been
dignified by wisdom, bravery, or virtue."

—SAMUEL JOHNSON.

"Old Bricks for Sale."

SUCH is the legend that catches one's eye, plain for all men to see, on many a hoarding in London streets. Behind those boards, wide or high, on which the callous contractor shamelessly blazons his dreadful trade—" Old Houses Bought to be Pulled Down "—he is stupidly pickaxing to pieces historic bricks and mortar which ought to be preserved priceless and imperishable. Within only a few years, I have had to look on, while thus were broken to bits and carted away to chaos John Dryden's dwelling-place in Fetter Lane, Benjamin Franklin's and Washington Irving's lodgings in Little Britain, Byron's birthplace in Hollis Street, Milton's "pretty garden-house," in Petty France, West-

minster. The spacious fireplace by which the
poet sat, during his fast-darkening days for
in this house he lost his first wife and his eye-
sight—was knocked down, as only one among
other numbered lots, to stolid builders. And
the stone, "Sacred to Milton, the Prince of
Poets"—placed in the wall facing the garden,
by William Hazlitt, living here early in our
century, beneath which Jeremy Bentham, occu-
pant of the adjoining house, was wont to make
his guests fall on their knees—this stone has
gone to "patch a wall to expel the winter's
flaw."

To this house there used to come, to call on
Hazlitt, a man of noticeable and impressive
presence:—small of stature, fragile of frame,
clad in clothing of tightly fitting black, which
was clerical as to cut and well-worn as to tex-
ture; his "almost immaterial legs," in Tom
Hood's phrase, ending in gaiters and straps;
his dark hair, not quite black, curling crisply
about a noble head and brow   "a head
worthy of Aristotle," Leigh Hunt tells us;
" full of dumb eloquence," are Hazlitt's words;
" such only may be seen in the finer portraits

of Titian," John Forster puts it; "a long,
melancholy face, with keen penetrating eyes,"
we learn from Barry Cornwall; brown eyes,
kindly, quick, observant; his dark complexion
and grave expression brightened by the frequent "sweet smile, with a touch of sadness
in it."

This visitor, of such peculiar and piquant
personality—externally "a rare composition of
the Jew, the gentleman, and the angel," to use
his own words of the singer Braham—is Charles
Lamb, a clerk in the East India House, living
with his sister Mary in chambers in the Inner
Temple. Let us walk with him as he returns to
those peaceful precincts, still of signal interest,
despite the ruin wrought by recent improve-
ments. Here, as in the day of Spenser, "stu-
dious lawyers have their bowers," and "have
thriven;" here, on every hand, we see the
shades of Evelyn, Congreve, Cowper, the
younger Colman, Fielding, Goldsmith, Johnson, Boswell; here, above all, the atmosphere
is still redolent with sweet memories of the
"best beloved of English writers," as Algernon
Swinburne well calls Charles Lamb. Closer

and more compact than elsewhere are his footprints in these Temple grounds; for he was
born within their gates, his youthful world was
bounded by their walls, his happiest years, as
boy and as man, were passed in their buildings.

And out beyond these borders we shall track
his steps mainly through adjacent streets, almost always along the City's streets, of which
he was as fond as Samuel Johnson or Charles
Dickens. He loved, all through life, " enchant-
ing London, whose dirtiest, drab-frequented
alley, and her lowest-bowing tradesman, I would
not exchange for Skiddaw, Helvellyn   .   .   .
O! her lamps of a night! her rich goldsmiths,
print-shops, toy-shops, mercers, hardware men,
pastry-cooks, St. Paul's Churchyard, the Strand,
Exeter 'Change, Charing Cross, with the man
upon a black horse! These are thy gods, O
London!" He couldn't care, he said, for the
beauties of nature, as they have been confinedly
called; and used to persist, with his pleasing
perversity, that when he climbed Skiddaw he
was thinking of the ham-and-beef shop in St.
Martin's Lane! " Have I not enough without
your mountains?" he wrote to Wordsworth.

" I do not envy you. I should pity you, did I
not know that the mind will make friends with
anything "—even with scenery ! It was a serious
step which Lamb took in later life, out from his
beloved streets into the country ; a step which
certainly saddened, and doubtless shortened, the
last stage of his earthly journey.

By a happy chance—for they have an unhal-
lowed habit in London town of destroying just
those buildings which I should select to save,
leaving unmolested those that would not be
missed, for all they ever have to say to us—
nearly every one of Lamb's successive homes
has been rescued from ruin, and kept inviolate
for our reverent regard. "Cheerful Crown
Office Row (place of my kindly engendure)"- -
to use his own words—has been only partly
rebuilt ; and that end of the block wherein lived
his parents stands almost in the same state as
when it was erected in 1737 ; this date told to
us to-day by the old-fashioned figures cut on
its easterly end. It was then named " The New
Building, opposite the Garden-Wall," and under
that division of the Chamber-Book of the Inner
Temple I have hunted up its numerous occu-

pants.   By this archive, and by the Books of
Accounts for the eighteenth century, I have
thus been enabled to trace Samuel Salt from
his first residence within the Temple in 1746, in
Ram Alley Building   now gone—through successive removals, until he settled down in his
last chambers, wherein he died in February,
1793.   The record reads—a " parliament "
meaning one of the fixed meetings in each term
of the Benchers of the Temple, for the purpose
of transacting business, and of calling students
to the bar—" 13th May, 1768.   At this Parliament : It is ordered that Samuel Salt, Esquire,
a Barrister of this Society, aged about Fifty, be
and is hereby admitted, for his own life, to the
benefit of an Assignment in and to All that
Ground Chamber, No. 2, opposite the Garden
Walk in Crown Office Row :   He, the said
Samuel Salt having paid for the Purchase
thereof into the Treasury of this Society, the
sum of One Hundred and Fifty pounds."

So that it was in No. 2—the numbers having
remained always unchanged—of Crown Office
Row, in one of the rear rooms of the ground
floor, which then looked out on Inner Temple

Lane, some of which rooms have been swept away since, and others have been slightly altered, that Charles Lamb was born, on the 10th February, 1775.

For Samuel Salt, Esquire—one of "The Old Benchers of the Inner Temple," whose pensive gentility is portrayed in Elia's essay of that title—had in his employ, as "his clerk, his good servant, his dresser, his friend, his 'flapper,' his guide, stop-watch, auditor, treasurer," one John Lamb; who formed, with his wife and children, the greater part of the household. Of him, too, under the well-chosen name of Lovel, we have the portrait, vivid and rounded, in his son's paper. "He was a man of an incorrigible and losing honesty. A good fellow withal and 'would strike.' In the cause of the oppressed he never considered inequalities, or calculated the number of his opponents. . . . Lovel was the liveliest little fellow breathing, had a face as gay as Garrick's, whom he was said greatly to resemble (I have a portrait of him which confirms it), possessed a fine turn for humorous poetry—next to Swift and Prior—moulded heads in clay or plaster of Paris to admiration.

by the dint of natural genius merely ; turned
cribbage-boards and such small cabinet toys, to
perfection ; took a hand at quadrille or bowls
with equal facility ; made punch better than
any man of his degree in England ; had the
merriest quips and conceits, and was altogether
as brimful of rogueries and inventions as you
could desire. He was a brother of the angle,
moreover, and just such a free, hearty, honest
companion as Mr. Izaak Walton would have
chosen to go a-fishing with."   In truth,

> " A merry cheerful man.   A merrier man,
> A man more apt to frame matter for mirth,
> Mad jokes and antics for a Christmas-eve,
> Making life social, and the laggard time
> To move on nimbly, never yet did cheer
> The little circle of domestic friends."

This John Lamb was devoted to the welfare
of his master, Samuel Salt ; who, in turn, did
nothing without consulting him, or failed in
anything without expecting and fearing his ad-
monishing. " He put himself almost too much
in his hands, had they not been the purest in
the world." To him and to his children Salt
was a life-long benefactor, and never, until death

had made an end to the good man's good
deeds, did there fall on the family any shadow
of change or trouble or penury.

It was in Salt's chambers that Charles and
his sister Mary, in their youthful years, "tum-
bled into a spacious closet of good old English
reading, and browsed at will on that fair and
wholesome pasturage:" thus already so early
drawn together by kindred tastes and studies,
even as they were already at one in their joint
heritage of the father's latent mental malady.
They had learned their letters, and picked up
crumbs of rudimentary knowledge, at a small
school in Fetter Lane, hard by the Temple;
the boys being taught in the mornings, the girls
in the afternoons. It stood on the edge of "a
discoloured, dingy garden in the passage leading into Fetter Lane from Bartlett's buildings.
This was near to Holborn." Bartlett's name is
still kept alive in Bartlett's Passage, right there ;
but no stone of his building now stands; and
the only growth of any garden in that turbu-
lent thoroughfare to-day is pavement and mud
and obscene urchins.

The inscription painted over their school-

door asserted that it was kept by " Mr. William Bird, Teacher of Mathematics and Languages." " Heaven knows what languages were
taught in it, then! I am sure that neither my
sister nor myself brought any out of it, but a
little of our native English "—so Charles wrote
nearly fifty years after to William Hone, the
editor of the *Every Day Book*. In its pages
had just appeared a woful narrative of the
poverty and desolation of one Starkey, who
had been " a gentle usher " in that school. In
the letter written by Lamb as a pendant to
that paper, he gossips characteristically about
the memories of those school-days thus awakened in him and in his sister. He vividly
portrays that down-trodden and downcast
usher, who " was not always the abject thing
he came to ;" and who actually had bold and
figurative words for the big girls, when they
talked together, or teased him during his recita-
tions. " Oh, how I remember our legs wedged
into those uncomfortable sloping desks, where
we sat elbowing each other ; and the injunc-
tions to attain a free hand, unattainable in
that position !"

They had, also, an aged school-dame here, who was proud to prattle to her pupils about her aforetime friend, Oliver Goldsmith; telling them how the good-natured man, then too poor to present her with a copy of his " Deserted Village," had lent it to her to read. He had become famous now, and so affluent—by the success of "The Good Natur'd Man," indeed!—that he had bought chambers on the second floor of No. 2 Brick Court, Middle Temple. This was but a biscuit toss from Crown Office Row, and perchance little Mary Lamb sometimes met, within the grounds, the short, stout, plain, pock-marked Irish doctor. He died in those chambers, only ten months before the birth of Charles; and was buried somewhere in the burying-ground of the Temple church. Within it, the Benchers put up a tablet to his memory. It is now in their vestry, wherein you shall also find the baptismal records of nearly all the Lamb children. The inscription on the tablet may have been first spelled out by Mary to her small and eager brother. Doubtless the two children knew the exact spot of his grave—

known exactly to none of us to-day—even as
they knew every corner and cranny of the
Temple grounds and buildings. They played
in its gardens, and looked down on them from
these same upper windows of No. 2 Crown
Office Row, which have been selected by Mr.
Fulleylove for his point of view. _Then_ these
gardens were as Shakespeare saw them, when
he, by a blameless anachronism, caused to be
enacted in them the famous scene of the
Roses; really rehearsed there, years before,
when Warwick assigned the rose to Planta-
genet. Now, the grounds have been extended
riverwards by the construction of the Embank-
ment; and the ancient historic blocks of buildings about them have been vulgarized into
something new and fine.

Mary and Charles were always together
during these early days. Of the seven children
born into the family, only three escaped death
in infancy: our two, and their brother John,
elder by two years than Mary. Their mother
loved them all, but most of all did she love
" dear, little, selfish, craving John; " who, as
was well written by Charles in later life, was

THE TEMPLE GARDENS, FROM CROWN OFFICE ROW.

not worthy of one-tenth of that affection which
Mary had a right to claim. But the mother,
like the father, was fond of fun, and found her
favourite in her handsome, sportive, noisy boy;
showing scant sympathy with and no insight
into the " moythered brains "—her own phrase
—of her sensitive, brooding daughter, who
already gave unheeded evidence of the congenital gloom by which her mind was to
become so clouded. Another member of the
small .household was the father's queer old-
maiden sister, Aunt Hetty, who passed her
days sitting silently or mumbling mysteriously
as she peered over her spectacles at the two
children, huddled together in their youthful
fear of her.

So it came to pass that Mary took charge of
the "weakly but very pretty babe "—as she recalled him, long years after, when he lay dead
at Edmonton, and she, in the next room, was
rambling disjointedly on about all their past.
With a childish wisdom, born, surely, not of
her years, but rather of her loneliness and her
unrequited caresses and her craving for companionship, she became at once his big sister,

his little mother, his guardian angel. She cared
for him in his helpless babyhood, she gave
strength to his feeble frame, she nurtured
his growing brain, she taught him to talk and
to walk. We seem to see the tripping of his
feet, that

> "—— half linger,
> Half run before,"

trying to keep pace with her steps then; even
as they always all through life tried to do,
wheresoever she walked, until they stopped at
the edge of his grave. The story of these two
lives of double singleness, from these childish
footprints to that grave, is simply the story of
their love. He, like his own Child-Angel, was
to know weakness and reliance and the shadow
of human imbecility; and he was to go with a
lame gait; *but, in his goings, he " exceeded all
mortal children in grace and swiftness."* And
so pity springs up in us, as in angelic bosoms;
and yearnings touch us, too, at the memory of
this "immortal lame one."

The boy's next school, to which he obtained a
presentation through the influence of Mr. Salt,
is known officially as Christ's Hospital, and is

commonly called the Blue-Coat School. It still
stands, a stately monument of the munificence
of " that godly and royal child, King Edward
VI., the flower of the Tudor name—the young
flower that was untimely cropped, as it began
to fill our land with its early odours—the boy-
patron of boys—the serious and holy child,
who walked with Cranmer and Ridley." To-
day, as we stay our steps in Newgate Street,
and peer through the iron railings at the dingy
red brick and stone facings of the ancient walls;
or, as we pause under the tiny statue of the
boy-king—founder, only ten days before his
death, of this noble hospital for poor fatherless
children and foundlings—we may look at the
out-of-school games going on in the great quad-
rangle : the foolish flapping skirts of the strip-
lings tucked into their red leathern waistbands
to give fair and free play to their lanky yellow
legs, their uncapped heads taking sun or shower
with equal unconcern.

Among them, unseen of them, seem to move
the forms of those other boys, Charles Lamb,
Samuel Taylor Coleridge, and Leigh Hunt—
all students here about this time. *Our* boy

2

was then a little past seven, a gentle, affectionate lad, "terribly shy," as he said of himself later, and made all the more sensitive
by his slight stammer, which lapsed to a stut-
ter when his nerves were wrought upon and
startled. Yet he was no more left alone and
isolated now than he was in after life; his
schoolfellows indulged him, the masters were
fond of him, and he was given special privileges
not known to the others. His little complaints
were listened to; he had tea and a hot roll o'
mornings; his ancient aunt used to toddle
there to bring him good things, when he,
schoolboy-like, only despised her for it, and, as
he confessed when older, used to be ashamed to
see her come and sit herself down on the old
coal-hole steps near where they went into the
grammar-school, and open her apron, and bring
out her basin, with some nice thing she had
caused to be saved for him. And he was
allowed to go home to the Temple for short
visits, from time to time, so passing his young
days between " cloister and cloister."

As he walks down the Old Bailey, or through
Fleet Market—then in the full foul odour of

A CORNER IN THE BLUE-COAT SCHOOL.

its wickedness and nastiness—and so up Fleet
Street on his way home, we may be sure that
his eager eye alights on all that is worth its
while, and that the young alchemist is already
putting into practice that process by which he
transmuted the mud of street and pavement
into pure gold, and so found all that was always
precious to him in their stones. After treading
them for many years, as boy and as man, he
asks: " Is any night-walk comparable to a walk
from St. Paul's to Charing Cross for lighting
and paving, for crowds going and coming without respite, the rattle of coaches, and the cheer-
fulness of shops?"

Among his schoolfellows, Charles formed
special friendships with a few select spirits;
and in Coleridge—"the inspired charity-boy,"
who entered the school at the same time,
though three years older—he found a life-long
companion. He looked up to the elder lad—
dreamy, dejected, lonely—with an affection and
a reverence which never failed all through life,
though in after years subject to the strain
of Coleridge's alienation, absence, and silence.
" Bless you, old sophist," he wrote once to Cole-

ridge, "who, next to human nature taught me all the corruption I was capable of knowing."

The two lads—along with Middleton, then a Grecian in the school, afterward Bishop of Calcutta—figure together in the fine group in silver which passes from ward to ward each year, according to merit in studies and in conduct. There is a Charles Lamb prize, too, given every year, as fittingly should be, to the best English essayist among the Blue-Coat boys, consisting of a silver medal: on one side a laurel wreath enwrapped about the hospital's arms; on the reverse, Lamb's profile, his hair something too curly, his aspect somewhat smug. It would be a solace to his kindly spirit could he know that his memory is thus kept green in the school which he left with sorrow, and to which he always looked back fondly. When a man, he used to go to see the boys; and Leigh Hunt— who entered a little later—has left us a pleasant picture of one of these visits. Charles had been a good student in the musty classical course of the school; not fonder of his hexameters than of his hockey, however; and when he left, in November, 1789, aged nearly fifteen,

he had become a deputy Grecian, he was a
capital Latin scholar, he probably had a firm
conviction that there was a language called
Greek, and he had read widely and well in the
English classics. Doubtless he was, even then,
already familiar with the Elizabethan dramatists, his life-long "midnight darlings;" above
all, he had nurtured himself upon the plays of
Shakespeare, which were " the strongest and
sweetest food of his mind from infancy."

The somewhat sombre surroundings of his
summer holidays, too, helped to form him into
an " old-fashioned child." The earliest thing he
could remember, he once wrote, was Mackery
End ; or Mackarel End, as it is spelled, perhaps
more properly, in some old maps of Hertfordshire. He could just recall his visit there, under the care of " Bridget Elia "—as he named
his sister in his essays. This youthful visit had
been made to a farmer, one Gladman, who had
married their grandmother's sister ; and his
farm-house was delightfully situated within a
gentle walk from Wheathampstead. Charles
describes his return thither with Mary, more
than forty years after ; and how, spite of their

trepidation as to the greeting they might get, they were joyfully received by a radiant woman-cousin, "who might have sat to a sculptor for the image of Welcome."

Mainly, however, were the boy's holidays passed with his grandmother Field, the old and trusted housekeeper of the Plumer family at Blakesware, in Hertfordshire: an ancient mansion, topped by many turrets, gables, carved chimneys, guarded all about by a solid red-brick wall and heavy iron gates. He was not allowed to go outside the grounds, and was content to wander over their trimly-kept terraces and about the tranquil park, wherein aged trees bent themselves in grotesque shapes. Beyond, he fancied that a dark lake stretched silently, striking terror to the lad's imagination.

"So strange a passion for the place possessed me in those years, that, though there lay—I shame to say how few roods distant from the mansion—half hid by trees, what I judged some romantic lake, such was the spell which bound me to the house, and such my carefulness not to pass its strict and proper precincts.

that the idle waters lay unexplored for me; and not till late in life, curiosity prevailing over elder devotion, I found, to my astonishment, a pretty brawling brook had been the Lacus Incognitus of my infancy." It was the placid tiny Ashe, which, curving about through this valley, here brawls over one of the wears that have given the place its name, and his lake proved to be only one of its little inlets.

Within doors he would wander through the wainscoted halls and the tapestried bedrooms —"tapestry so much better than painting, not adorning merely, but peopling the wainscots . . . . all Ovid on the walls, in colours vivider than his descriptions. Actæon in mid sprout, with the unappeasable prudery of Diana; and the still more provoking, and almost culinary, coolness of Dan Phœbus, eel-fashion, deliberately divesting of Marsyas." He would gaze long in wonder on the busts of the Twelve Cæsars ranged around the marble hall, and would study the prints of Hogarth's Progress of the Rake and of the Harlot hung on the walls. "Why, every plank and panel of that house for me had magic in it," he says in the essay on

" Blakesmoor in H——shire;" under which name he disguises the place. That is a delightful paper, ending with this most musical passage: " Mine too—whose else? —thy costly fruit-garden, with its sun-baked southern wall; the ampler pleasure-garden, rising backwards from the house in triple terraces, with flower-pots now of palest lead, save that a speck here and there, saved from the elements, bespake their pristine state to have been gilt and glittering; the verdant quarters backwarder still; and, stretching still beyond, in old formality, thy firry wilderness, the haunt of the squirrel, and the day-long murmuring wood-pidgeon, with that antique image in the centre, God or Goddess I wist not; but child of Athens or old Rome paid never a sincerer worship to Pan or to Sylvanus in their native groves, than I to that fragmental mystery."

Lamb went back in 1822 to revisit these boyhood scenes, only to find that ruin had been done with a swift hand, and that brick-and-mortar knaves had plucked every panel and spared no plank. The ancient mansion entirely disappeared during that year, and a new Blakesware House soon after rose on its site : "worthy in picturesque architecture and fair proportions of its old namesake," in the words of Canon Ainger.

The boy used to go to church of a Sunday with his grandmother, to Widford ; nearer to their place than their own parish church at Ware. On a stone under the noble elms many a transatlantic visitor has read the simple inscription, " Mary Field. August 5th, 1792." Beneath it lies the grandmother.

II.

UNTIL lately, in the year 1889, when the frenzy for Improvement and the rage for Rent wiped it out, I could have shown you a queer bit of cobble wall, set in and thus saved from ruin by the new wall of the Metal Exchange. These few square feet of stone were the sole remaining relic of the chapel of the old manor-house of Leadenhall—so named from its roofing of lead, rare in those days—which house had been presented to the City of London by the munificent Richard Whittington in 1408, to be used as a granary and market. It escaped the Great Fire, and its chapel was not torn down until June, 1812. This piece of its wall, having been preserved then, was built in with, and so formed part of, the old East India House. That famous structure stretched its stately and severe façade along Leadenhall Street just beyond Gracechurch Street, and so around the corner into Lime Street. It was, withal, a gloomy

THE EAST INDIA HOUSE.

[From an old print in the British Museum.]

pile, with its many-columned Ionic portico.
Its pediment contained a stone sovereign of
Great Britain, holding an absurd umbrella-
shaped shield over the sculptured figures of
eastern commerce ; its front was dominated
by Britannia comfortably seated, at her right
Europe, on a horse, and at her left Asia, on
a camel.

Within its massive walls –holding memories
of Warren Hastings and of Cornwallis, of Mill,
gathering material for his history of India, and
of Hoole, translating Tasso in leisure hours –
were spacious halls and lofty rooms, statues and
pictures, a museum of countless curiosities from
the East.   Beneath were vaults stored with a
goodly share of the wealth of Ormus and of Ind,
and dungeons wherein were found—on the
downfall of John Company, in 1860, and the
destruction of his fortress a little later—chains
and fetters, and a narrow passage leading to a
concealed postern : these last for the benefit
of the victims of John's press-gang, entrapped,
drugged, shipped secretly down the river, and
so sent across water to serve Clive and Coote
as food for powder.

Upstairs, at a desk, sat Charles Lamb, keeping accounts in big books during " thirty-three years of slavery," as he phrased it : of unfailing and untiring—albeit not untired—devotion to his duties, as his employers well knew.   It was in April, 1792, just as he became seventeen, that he was first chained to this hard desk; and it came about in this way.

John Lamb, the father, had got nearly to his dotage and quite to uselessness, and was pensioned off by his master about this period.   The elder brother, dear little selfish, craving John, had grown into a broad, burly, jovial bachelor, wedded to his own ways; living an easy life apart from them all; "marching in quite an opposite direction," as his brother kindly puts it—speaking, as was his wont, not without tenderness for him.   He contributed nothing to the support of the family, and Mary added but little, beyond her own meagre maintenance by dress-making on a small scale—a trade she had taught herself.   In her article on needlework, written in 1814, for the *British Lady's Magazine*, she says : " In early life I passed eleven years in the exercise of my needle for a liveli-

hood." And so it seemed needful that the
boy, not yet fifteen years old on leaving
Christ's, should get to work to eke out the
family's scanty income.

John Lamb had a comfortable position in the
South Sea House. It stood where now stands
the Oriental Bank, at the end of Threadneedle
Street, as you turn up into Bishopsgate Within:
"its magnificent portals ever gaping wide,
and disclosing to view a grave court, with
cloisters and pillars." In his essay entitled
"The South Sea House," Lamb has drawn the
picture of the place within: its "stately por-
ticos, imposing staircases, offices roomy as the
state apartments in palaces; . . . the oaken
wainscots hung with pictures of deceased gov-
ernors; . . . huge charts, which subsequent
discoveries have antiquated; dusty maps of
Mexico, dim as dreams; and soundings of the
Bay of Panama!" All "long since dissipated
or scattered into air at the blast of the breaking
of that famous BUBBLE."

Here Charles was given a desk, and here
he worked, but at what work and with what
wage we do not know. It was not for many

months, however, for he soon received his
appointment in the East India House through
the kindness of Samuel Salt—the final kindness that came to the family from their
aged well-doer; for he died during that year,
1792. The young accountant had but little
taste for, and still less knowledge of, the mercantile mysteries over which he was set to
toil. He knew less geography than a schoolboy of six weeks' standing, he said in mature
manhood ; and a map of old Ortelius was as au-
thentic as Arrowsmith to him. Of history and
chronology he possessed some vague points,
such as he could not help picking up in the
course of his miscellaneous reading; but he
never deliberately sat down to study any chronicle of any country ! His friend Manning once,
with great painstaking, got him to think that
he understood the first proposition in Euclid,
but gave him over in despair at the second.
And, toil as toughly as he might over his accounts, he had to own, after years of adding,
that "I think I lose £100 a year at the India
House, owing solely to my want of neatness in
making up my accounts."

And yet, just the more uncongenial as was his labour, by just so much more did it tend in all ways to his good. Wordsworth said truly, with admirable acumen, that Lamb's submission to this mechanical employment placed him in fine contrast with other men of genius—his contemporaries—who, in sacrificing personal independence, made a wreck of their morality and honour. No such wreck did Charles Lamb make, and his peculiar pride prevented his sacrificing ever one iota of his independence. He could be no man's debtor nor dependant, and was content to cut his coat to suit his cloth, all his life long. His sole hatred, curiously enough, was for bankrupts; and he has portrayed with delicious irony, in his essay, " The Two Races of Men "—the men who borrow and the men who lend—the contempt of the former for money, " accounting it (yours and mine especially) no better than dross !"

The new clerk began with an annual salary of £70, to be increased by a small sum each year. Many huge account-books were filled with his figures who knows what has become of them?

and these he used to call his real works, filling
some hundred folios on the shelves in Leadenhall Street. His printed books, he claimed,
were the solace and the recreations of his
out-of-office hours at home.

NO. 7 LITTLE QUEEN STREET.

That home was no
longer in the Temple.
The home there, of
" snug firesides, the
low-built roof, par-
lours ten feet by ten,
frugal board, and all
the homeliness of
home," had been
given up, on the
death of Mr. Salt;
or, it may be, even
earlier, for I am un-
able to fix the date.
The family had moved into poor lodgings, at
No. 7 Little Queen Street, Holborn, where
we find them during the year 1795. The site
of this house, and of its adjoining neighbours
on both sides, Nos. 6 and 8, is now occupied
by Holy Trinity Church of Lincoln's Inn

Fields. The first house of the old row still standing is No. 9, and the side entrance of the Holborn Restaurant is No. 5; so that, you see, the windows of the Lamb lodgings looked out directly down Gate Street, their house exactly facing the western embouchure of that short and narrow street.

I pass in front of the little church a score of times in a month, and each time I look with gladness at its ugly front, content that it has replaced the walls within which was enacted that terrible tragedy of September, 1796. The family was straitened direfully in means, and in miserable case in many ways; the mother ailing helplessly, the father decaying rapidly in mind and body; the aged aunt, more of a burden than a help, despite the scanty board she paid; and the sister, suffering almost ceaselessly from attacks of her congenital gloom, submitting to the constant toil of her household duties, of her dressmaking, and of nursing her parents. Early in 1796 Charles wrote to Coleridge: "My life has been somewhat diversified of late. The six weeks that finished last year and began this, your very humble

3

servant spent very agreeably in a mad-house at Hoxton. I am got somewhat rational now, and don't bite any one. But mad I was!" This was his only attack; there was no more such agreeable diversity in his life, and he was cured by the most heroic of remedies.

In the *London Times* of Monday, September 26, 1796—in which issue the editors "exult in the isolation and cutting off" of the various armies of the French Republic in Germany, and doubt the "alleged successes of the army in Italy reported to the Directory by General Buonaparte;" in which the Right Honourable John, Earl of Chatham, is named Lord President of His Majesty's Most Honourable Privy Council; and in which "Mr. Knowles, nephew and pupil of the late Mr. Sheridan," advertises that he has "opened an English, French, and Latin preparatory school for a limited number of young gentlemen at No. 15 Brompton Crescent"—in this journal appeared the following:

"On Friday afternoon, the coroner and a jury sat on the body of a lady in the neighbourhood of Holborn, who died in consequence of a wound from her daughter the preceding day.

It appeared, by the evidence adduced, that, while the family were preparing for dinner, the young lady seized a case-knife lying on the table, and in a menacing manner pursued a little girl, her apprentice, around the room. On the calls of her infirm mother to forbear, she renounced her first object, and with loud shrieks, approached her parent.   The child, by her cries, quickly brought up the landlord of the house, but too late. The dreadful scene presented to him the mother lifeless, pierced to the heart, on a chair, her daughter yet wildly standing over her with the fatal knife, and the old man, her father, weeping by her side, himself bleeding at the forehead from the effects of a severe blow he had received from one of the forks she had been madly hurling about the room.

" For a few days prior to this, the family had observed some symptoms of insanity in her, which had so much increased on the Wednesday evening that her brother, early the next morning, went to Dr. Pitcairn : but that gentleman was not at home.

" It seems that the young lady had been once

before deranged. The jury, of course, brought in their verdict—*Lunacy*."

The *True Briton* said: "It appears that she had been before in the earlier part of her life deranged, from the harassing fatigues of too much business. As her carriage toward her mother had always been affectionate in the extreme, it is believed her increased attachment to her, as her infirmities called for it by day and by night, caused her loss of reason at this time. It has been stated in some of the morning papers that she has an insane brother in confinement; but this is without foundation."

I ask you to notice with what decent reticence, so far from the ways, and so foolish in the eyes, of our modern journalistic shamelessness, all the names are suppressed in this report. It is certain that it would not be looked on with favour in the office of any enterprising journal, nowadays! One error the reporter did make; it was not the landlord, but Charles, who came at the child's cries; luckily at hand just in time to disarm his sister. and thus prevent further harm.

So he was at hand from that day on. all

through his life, holding her and helping her
in the frequent successive returns of her
wretched malady. His gentle, loving, resolute
soul proved its fine and firm fibre under the
strain of more than forty years of undeviating
devotion to which I know no parallel. He
quietly gave up all other ties and cares and
pleasures for this supreme duty; he never for
one hour remitted his vigil; he never repined
or posed, he never even said to himself that
he was doing something fine. And such is
the potency of this intangible tonic of unsel-
fish self-sacrifice, that *his* tremulous nerves
grew tenser under its action, and his reason
relaxed her rule thenceforward never any
more. The poor guiltless murderess was sent
by the authorities to an asylum at Hoxton.
There John Lamb and their friends thought
it best to isolate her, safely and quietly, for
life, spite of her intervals of sanity; but,
from the outset, Charles fought against this,
offered his life-long personal guardianship—this
boy of twenty-two, with only £100 a year!
—and at length succeeded in squeezing con-
sent from the crown officials. He counts

up, in a letter to Coleridge, the coin " Daddy
and I " can spare for Mary, and computes all
the care she will bring: " I know John will
make speeches about it, *but she shall not go into
an hospital.*" So he meets her as she comes
out, and they walk away through life hand in
hand, even as they used to walk through the
fields many a time in later years on the approach of one of her repeated relapses ; he leading her back to temporary retirement in the
asylum, hand in hand together, both silently
crying !

The mother's body is laid in the graveyard of
St. Andrew's, Holborn, the aunt is sent to other
relatives, and the father's wound having speed-
ily healed, Charles removed with him to lodgings at No. 45 Chapel Street, Pentonville, on
the corner of Liverpool Road. It was a plain
little wooden house, as you may see it portrayed in the cut copied from W. Carew Hazlitt's "Charles and Mary Lamb." Now, there
stands in its place a blazing brazen "pub,"
quite in keeping with the squalid street. Its
bar, like that favourite bar of Newman Noggs,
" faces both ways," in a hopeless attempt to

cope all around with the unquenchable thirst
of that quarter!

The new home, however, brought but slight
brightening to the gloom and horror from
which Charles
had fled in the
old home. It
was shadowed by
the almost ac-
tual presence of
the dead mother,
and made even
more dismal by
the living ghost
of the aged fa-
ther, now " in the
decay of his facul-
ties, palsy-smit-
ten, in the last
sad stage of hu-

THE HOUSE AT PENTONVILLE.

man weakness, a remnant most forlorn of what
he was." He was released by death early in
1799, and laid by his wife's side in the burying-ground of St. Andrew's, Holborn; the
ground since then having been cut through and

wiped out by the construction of the Holborn viaduct.

Old Aunt Hetty, "the kindest, goodest creature," had come back to them, but only to die; and their faithful servant, who had followed their fortunes and their misfortunes, sickened slowly unto death. Mary had been allowed to return home for a while, from the rooms at Hackney, where Charles had placed her on her release from the asylum, and where he passed his Sundays and holidays with her. Now, she again broke down, and was forced to go back into seclusion at Hoxton. Then, for the one time in all his life, Charles gave way under these successive strokes, and made his only moan in a letter to Coleridge, early in 1800: "Mary, in consequence of fatigue and anxiety, is fallen ill again, and I was obliged to remove her yesterday. I am left alone in a house, with nothing but Hetty's dead body to keep me company. To-morrow I bury her, and then I shall be quite alone, with nothing but a cat to remind me that the house has been full of living beings like myself. My heart is quite sunk, and I don't know where to look for

relief. Mary will get better again, but her constantly being liable to these attacks is dreadful;
nor is it the least of our evils that her case and
all our story is so well known around us. We
are in a manner *marked.* . . . I am going
to try and get a friend to come and be with me
to-morrow—I am completely shipwrecked."

No, he was not completely wrecked, but terribly tempest-tossed for a time; and so at last
—in the high phrase of Coleridge—"called by
sorrow and anguish and a strange desolation of
hopes into quietness."

But "marked" cruelly was the little family
in very truth. Soon they were forced to make
one more of their many repeated removes.
Other quarters were offered them just then in
the house of one John Mathew Gutch, who had
been a schoolmate at Christ's of Lamb's, and
was at that time a law stationer in Southampton Buildings, Holborn. It was a most
friendly and even generous offer, for Gutch
knew the whole sad story, and the dangers, in
all probability, portending. His house has been
torn down only lately, along with the one hard
by in which lived Hazlitt, twenty years later.

It would be but the dreariest of records of
the young clerk's three years at Pentonville,
and of his earlier life in Little Queen Street, if
one could point to nothing brighter than his
anxiety, poverty, loneliness; his dull days at
his desk, his duller evenings at cribbage with
his almost imbecile father. " I go home at
night over-wearied, quite faint, and then to
cards with my father, who will not let me
enjoy a meal in peace." For he says—and to
the son this is unanswerable!—" If you won't
play with me, you might as well not come
home at all." He is not allowed to write a
letter, he can go nowhere, he has no acquaintance. " No one seeks or cares for my society,
and I am left alone." The only literary man
he knew was George Dyer; who was "goodness itself," indeed, but not a stimulating companion. Sometimes he succeeded in slipping
out to the theatre, of which he was as fond
as, when a boy, he felt the delights he has
delineated in " My First Play." These came
back with added keenness to him now, after a
long interval; for the scholars at Christ's had
not been allowed to enter any play-house.

And there was solace for all his privations
to be found in his beloved books, and he
" browsed" in many a field. "I have no re-
pugnances. Shaftesbury is not too genteel for
me, nor Jonathan Wild too low. I can read
anything which I call *a book*. There are things
in that shape which I cannot allow for such."
He had a spiritual kinship with the Eliza-
bethans, and was worthy, in his own words, of
listening to Shakespeare read aloud one of his
scenes hot from his brain. Yet he was fond of
the writers of the last century, and wished that
he might be able to forget Fielding and Swift
and the rest for the sake of reading them anew.
For modern literature, save for a few favourite
poems and for the works of his personal friends,
he cared but little. For modern affairs he
cared nothing, and knew nearly nothing about
them. There is hardly a hint in his letters of
the grim Napoleonic drama which was enacted
during the younger years of the century; he
only grieved that War and Nature and Mr. Pitt
should have conspired to increase the cost of
coals and bread and beer! He once heard a
butcher in the market-place of Enfield say

something about a change of ministry ; and it
struck him that he neither knew nor cared who
was in and who was out. Indeed, he could
not make these present times present to himself, and lived in the past, so that the so-
called realities of life seemed its mockeries
to him. "Hang the age! I will write for an-
tiquity," he told the able editor who criticised
his style as not in keeping with the taste of the
age. In truth, he was a walking anachronism,
and beneath his nineteenth-century waistcoat
pulsated a heart of the seventeenth century—
that of Sir Thomas Browne, perchance.

Lamb's first appearance in print was made
anonymously during these dreary days, in the
Morning Chronicle, and consisted of a sonnet
to Mrs. Siddons, whom he had seen for the
first time, and who had profoundly impressed
him. This sonnet and three others formed his
share of a small volume of "Poems on Various
Subjects," mainly by Coleridge, issued under
the latter's name in the spring of 1796. His
preface says: "The effusions signed C. L. were
written by Mr. Charles Lamb of the India
House. Independently of the signature, their

superior merit would have sufficiently distinguished them." In the summer of 1797 ap
peared a second edition, "to which are now
added poems by Charles Lamb and Charles
Lloyd"—the former contributing about fifteen
short poems. This Lloyd was the son of a Birmingham banker, a morbid young man addicted
to rhyme and to melancholy—a recent acquaintance of Lamb's, and one who could not have
been a cheerful comrade for him, just then.

In 1798 appeared "A Tale of Rosamund Gray
and Old Blind Margaret," as its original title
ran. It is the best known of his works after
his essays, and we all echo Shelley's words to
Leigh Hunt: "What a lovely thing is 'Rosamund Gray'! How much knowledge of the
sweetest and deepest part of our nature in it!"
And yet this "miniature romance," as Talfourd
well named it, surely seems somewhat unreal
and artificial, for all its charm!

Lamb found constant comfort, too, during
these dark years, in his only two intimate
friends: Coleridge, with whom he had renewed
his companionship, broken by Coleridge's visit to
Germany, and by his six months' service in the

Light Dragoons; and Southey, whose healthy
and wholesome common-sense was just then a
timely tonic for Lamb. These three youthful
dreamers used to sit and smoke and speculate of
nights in a little den at the back of the *Salutation and Cat*—a tavern at No. 17 Newgate
Street, nearly opposite the old School. Two of
them may haply have learned their way there
while still scholars ! " I image to myself that
little smoky room at the *Salutation and Cat*,
where we have sat together through the winter
nights, beguiling the cares of life with poesy,"
Lamb wrote, later; and he refers more than
once to " that nice little smoky room at the
Salutation, which is even now continually pre-
senting itself to my recollection, with all its
associated train of pipes, tobacco, egg-hot,
welsh-rabbit, metaphysics, and poetry." They
say that the wary landlord, to whom Coleridge's
rhapsodies were quite unintelligible, yet who
fully understood their value in drawing a knot
of thirsty listeners, offered the Talker free
quarters for life, if he would stay and talk !

The men who sit and smoke and soak in tap-
rooms, and who never know when they are

full in any sense, are just the sort to find copi-
ous refreshment in such eternal monologue.
Carlyle's concise dictum thereanent would have
fallen flat on their pendulous ears: " To sit as
a passive bucket and be pumped into, whether
one like it or not, can in the end be exhilarat-
ing to no creature!"

The old tavern—so old, that within its walls
Sir Christopher Wren used to sit often with his
pipe, coming in tired from the rebuilding of St.
Paul's, just around the corner—has itself been
rebuilt, the little smoky room is wiped out, the
Cat has vanished, and the *Salutation* greets
us as a slap-bang City eating-house and bar.
Before the destruction of the original inn, an
old fellow, who had been a Grecian in Lamb's
time, used to hobble up the entrance-way, once
a year, when he came to some great function of
the Blue-Coats, and look longingly into that
once " murmurous haunt " through the glass
door. Invited to enter one day, he stood in
the smoking-room for a while, his eyes wet and
his voice husky ; then he went away, never to
reappear. Doubtless he had drunk and smoked
through many of those "O noctes cœnœque

Deûm! Anglice Welsh rabbit, punch, and poesy," in Lamb's words.

Another favourite resort of the three cronies was *The Feathers*, a dirty, dingy, delightful tavern, as I have seen it, in Hand Court, Holborn, nearly opposite the Great Turnstile leading into Lincoln's Inn Fields. It was only two minutes' walk from the lodgings in Little Queen Street, and but a few houses distant from the oil-shop of Charles's godfather, at the corner of Featherstone Buildings and Holborn. *The Feathers* has gone to its own place, a modern something maddens me on its site, and all that I have been able to rescue is the quaint sign which hung until lately above the entrance of the court in Holborn, and looked down on the frequent goings in and out of our friends.

It was while living in Pentonville that Lamb passed through his second, and his final, love-sickness. His first attack had been caused by undue exposure, when a guileless youth, unprotected by proper prophylactics, to the provocative charms of the " Alice Winterton " of his later writings. It is believed that her real name was Ann Simmons, and that he used to meet

THE FEATHERS TAVERN.

her during his holidays at his grandmother's place. For, with all his delightful egoistic frankness in prattling about himself, *this* was the one point too tender to be touched on, seriously or jocularly, ever to any one. It is of her, surely, that he is thinking in two of his four sonnets in the Coleridge collection, wherein he speaks of his "fancied wanderings with a fair-haired maid." He placed the scene of "Rosamund Gray" in the cottage where lived Ann Simmons, near Widford, not far from Blakesware; and they show to sentimental strangers that portion of the cluster of cottages still left. They claim that it is her portrait which he drew for that of his heroine even as he is the Allan Clare of the little story. He certainly hints, just for once, at this love scrape in that letter to Coleridge in which he speaks of his six weeks' stay in the Hoxton Asylum: "It may convince you of my regard for you when I tell you that my head ran on you in my madness, as much almost as on another person, who I am inclined to think was the more immediate cause of my temporary frenzy." But his recovery from

4

both derangements was radical and permanent,
and he was able to say, only a little later: " I
am pleased and satisfied with myself that this
weakness troubles me no longer. I am wedded,
Coleridge, to the fortunes of my sister and my
poor old father." That wedding to the fortunes of his sister *was* his life-long union, and
haply saved him from any other, which would
have harmed, rather than have helped, this
man ; and would have sacrificed deplorably *this*
vivid personality on the altar of the greatly-
glorified god, the infestive Humdrum.

His serene good sense asserted its strength,
at no time and in no way, so signally as in his
absolute emancipation from this transient en-
slavement ; and in his sedate statement of the
fact—true in so many cases where the victim is
too stupid to know it or too timorous to own it
—that, " if it drew me out of some vices, it also
prevented the growth of many virtues."

As is usual, however, with the amatory in-
firmity, he suffered from that slight and super-
ficial relapse, later in life, to which I have
already referred. In his daily goings to and
fro in Islington, he used to meet the lovely

Quakeress, to whom he never spoke, and whom
he adored silently and from afar.　He only knew
that she was named Hester, and it is her name
which he has made immortal and her sweet
memory which he has embalmed imperishably
in his exquisite verses:

"When maidens such as Hester die."

And his first, his serious, affair may have justi-
fied its existence by recalling to us his well-
known wish that no incident, no untoward acci-
dent even, of his life might have been reversed.
So it is, that in his " New Year's Eve" he avers
that " it is better that I should have pined
away seven of my goldenest years, when I was
thrall to the fair hair and fairer eyes of Alice
W——n, than that so passionate a love-adven-
ture should be lost."

III

"I AM going to change my lodgings, having received a hint that it would be agreeable, at Our Lady's next feast. I have partly fixed upon most delectable rooms, which look out (when you stand a-tiptoe) over the Thames and Surrey Hills, at the upper end of King's Bench Walk, in the Temple. There I shall have all the privacy of a house without the encumbrance, and shall be able to lock my friends out, as often as I desire to hold free converse with any immortal mind—for my present lodgings resemble a minister's levée, I have so increased my acquaintance (as they call 'em) since I have resided in town." In this letter, written to Manning early in 1801, three significant points call for comment. The phrase " in town," referring to his residence in Southampton Buildings, shows how his previous abode in Islington was then in the country, and how the squalid houses of the foul Chapel Street of to-day have supplanted those pleasant cottages set in gardens, with rural lanes cutting the fields between. His curt reference to their "having received a hint" to move, proves how pitifully they were "marked," as he had already put it, and how soon even the kindly Gutch withdrew his offer of shelter. The few words, "I have so increased my acquaintance" give a wide suggestion of the already growing attraction of this odd, original young character to all bright minds and sweet natures with whom he came in contact.

And so, on Lady Day, March 25, 1801, he and Mary moved into the Temple, there to begin, near their childhood home, that life of "dual loneliness," never again broken in upon: consoled by their mutual affection, cheered by their common tastes, brightened by the companionship of congenial beings. In the Temple they remained for seventeen years, living in two sets of chambers during that period. After eight years' abode at No. 16 Mitre Court Buildings, they were compelled to quit, their landlord wanting the rooms for himself. Towards the end of March, 1809, in a letter to Manning, then

in China, Lamb wrote as if he were in the next
street : "While I think of it, let me tell you
we are moved.   Don't come any more to Mitre
Court Buildings.   We are at 34 Southampton
Buildings, Chancery Lane, and shall be here
till about the end of May, when we remove to
No. 4 Inner Temple Lane, where I mean to
live and die."

Their home in Southampton Buildings during these few months while changing chambers
still stands intact ; a delightful old square, solid,
brick house, just in front of the tiny garden of
Staple Inn.   But both blocks of buildings in
which he lived during those seventeen years
in the Temple have been torn down and replaced by modern structures.

Although he disliked leaving the old chambers, he found the new set, on the third and
fourth floors of No. 4 Inner Temple Lane,
"far more commodious and roomy. . . . The
rooms are delicious, and the best look back
into Hare Court, where there is a pump always
going. Just now it is dry. Hare Court trees
come in at the window, so that it is like living
in a garden!"   This was written to Coleridge,

in June, 1809; and to Manning, in letters during this period, Lamb spoke of the churchyard-
like court having "three trees and a pump in
it. Do you know it? I was born near it,
and used to drink at that pump when I was a
Rechabite of six years old . . . the water
of which is excellent cold, with brandy, and not
very insipid without. Here I hope to set up
my rest and not quit till Mr. Powell, the un-
dertaker, gives me notice that I may have possession of my last lodging. He lets lodgings
for single gentlemen. . . . I should be
happy to see you any evening. Bring any of
your friends, the Mandarins, with you."

He did, indeed, as he often complained, hate
and dread unaccustomed places, but he was
well content to discover that this new habita-
tion had "more aptitudes for growing old than
you shall often see."

It was here that Mary made the memorable
find of an empty adjoining garret of four un-
tenanted, unowned rooms; of which they took
possession by degrees, and to which Charles
could escape from his too frequent friends, who
had more leisure than himself. Here he did

his literary work in secrecy and silence, "as
much alone as if he were in a lodging in the
midst of Salisbury Plain." They never knew to
whom these chambers rightly belonged, and they
were never dispossessed. So all was well with
him, and even in his whimsical perversity he was
able to complain only that there was another
" Mr. Lamb" not far from him ; " his duns and
his girls frequently stumble up to me, and I am
obliged to satisfy both in the best way I am able."

The staircase of the new building is still
stumbled up by duns and girls, you may drink
from that same pump to-day, you may see those
trees still in that court, but *his* windows no
longer look out on trees and pump and court.

Talfourd and Procter have left vivid pictures
of the memorable Wednesday evenings in the
Temple, the former contrasting them with the
stately assemblages of Holland House. " Like
other great men, I have a public day," Lamb
wrote. He loved men, and he had a rare ca-
pacity for getting at the best they had in them,
a real reverence for their abilities, a kindly sympathy with their diverse tastes, and a most
friendly frankness as to all their foibles. " How

could I hate him?" he asked of some one: "Don't I know him? I never could hate any one I knew." He looked so constantly and so closely into the strange faces of calamity, that he yearned always for the nearness of friendly features. Above all, he understood, as Goethe did, "how mighty is the goddess of propinquity;" and although he was so untiring and prolific and delightful in his letters to absent friends, he insisted that "one glimpse of the human face and one shake of the human hand is better than whole reams of this thin, cold correspondence; yea, of more worth than all the letters that have sweated the fingers of sensibility from Madame Sévigné and Balzac to Sterne and Shenstone."

So it came to pass that his little rooms in the Temple held a motley crowd. Low-browed rooms they were, set about with worn, homely, home-like furniture; his favourite books—his sole extravagance—in their shelves all about. His ragged veterans, he called them; "the finest collection of shabby books I ever saw; such a number of first-rate works in very bad condition is, I think, nowhere to be found," is

Crabb Robinson's caustic comment on them. In narrow black frames, on the walls of his best room, hung "a choice collection of the works of Hogarth, an English painter of some humour." The sideboard was already spread by Mary with cold beef, porter, punch; tobacco and pipes were at hand, and tables made ready for whist. This is Charles's invitation: "Swipes exactly at nine, punch to commence at ten, *with argument;* difference of opinion expected to take place about eleven; perfect unanimity with some haziness and dimness before twelve!" He used to play right through his programme. His old cronies came, "friendly harpies," he named many of them: for, as he said of the pretended dead Elia, his intimados were, to confess a truth, in the world's eye, a ragged regiment. He never forsook a friend, ragged or rich in raiment or in repute, and "the burrs stuck to him; but they were good and loving burrs for all that." It was the simple statement of a truth which he had made, long before this: "I cannot scatter friendships like chuck-farthings, nor let them drop from mine hand, like hour-glass sand."

New acquaintances came, too ; never men of
fame or fortune or fashion, but men of mark,
you may be sure. And many among them
notable only for some tincture of the absurd
in their characters : for " I love a *Fool*," he
said, "as naturally as if I were of kith and
kin to him." Crabb Robinson has left us his
reminiscence of this place and these people,
when speaking of his first acquaintance with
the Lambs : " They were then living in a garret in Inner Temple Lane. In that humble
apartment I spent many happy hours, and
saw a greater number of excellent persons
than I had ever seen collected together in one
room." Thus has he summed up, in his sedate
way, all that need be said on that score.

The capricious Coleridge had once more become constant, after his refusal for two years to
write, and his needless estrangement, which had
called forth Lamb's lines, " I had a friend, a
kinder friend had no man ; " and of whom, after
many years, he yet was able to say : " The
more I see of him in the quotidian undress and
relaxation of his mind, the more cause I see to
love him and believe him a very good man."

There was Hazlitt—trying to paint when Lamb
first met him, finding later his true calling as
art critic and essayist ; easily first of all in that
field, before or after him, in insight, breadth,
and vigour ; arrogant, intense, bitter, brooding
forever over the fall of Napoleon : the only
male creature he reverenced except Coleridge.
He must needs respect, in Coleridge, the one
man known to him who alone could surpass
him in untiring fluency, even under the influence of strongest tea—sole stimulus allowed
himself by Hazlitt at that time.   Him, Lamb
finds to be, " in his natural state, one of the
wisest and finest spirits breathing."   And he,
too, had tried to quarrel with the Lambs, and
had failed, as did all who made the sorry attempt !   There was William Wordsworth, as-
cetic, self-centred, quite sure of himself ; whose
true powers, and all that was genuine in his
genius, Lamb was one of the first to recognize
and to celebrate.   There was Godwin, so bold
in his speculations, so daring with his pen, so
placid in person, and so mild of voice.   This
terrifying radical used to prattle on trivial
topics till after supper, and then invariably

fall fast asleep. ".A very well-behaved decent man, . . . quite a tame creature, I assure you; a middle-sized man, both in stature and understanding." wrote his keen-eyed host. There was old Captain Burney, afterward admiral, son of the famous organist, brother of the more famous writing-woman, Fanny, Madame d'Arblay. He had been taught by Eugene Aram, he had sailed all around the globe with Captain Cook, and was still young and tender in heart under his rough exterior. There was his son, Martin, of whom Lamb said, "I have not found a whiter soul than thine;" Leigh Hunt, airy, sprightly, full of fine fancies; Charles Lloyd, poetic and intense; Tom Hood, slight of figure, feeble of voice, face of a Methodist parson, silent save for his sudden puns; Thomas Manning, the Cambridge mathematical tutor, "a man of a thousand;" Basil Montagu, the philanthropized courtier; stalwart Allan Cunningham; Haydon, the painter, eager everywhere for controversy; the preacher, Edward Irving, content to listen, there; Bernard Barton, Quaker poet, bank drudge; gentle and genial Barry Cornwall; Talfourd, the sympathetic chronicler of these scenes; constant and trusty Crabb Robinson; De Quincey, self-involved and sometimes spiteful, yet not behind any one of that brilliant band in his love for Lamb, whom he earnestly attests to be " the noblest of human beings."

There appeared sometimes at these gatherings a most curious character, hardly known now as one of this group, but remembered rather from the parts he plays in the pages of Bulwer and of Dickens. This was Thomas Wainewright, the " Janus Weathercock " of the *London Magazine;* a flimsy, plausible, conceited scoundrel, in whom Lamb good-naturedly found something to like. It was after our friend's death that Wainewright's thefts and poisonings brought him to trial, and sent him to Van Diemen's land, where the dandy convict died in madness, raving and unrepentant.

And Charles Lamb, the central and dominating personality of all these strong characters, towers above them all, not only and not so much by the greatness of his gifts as by that of his character. For simplicity, sincerity,

singleness of soul—all that is childlike in genius
—all those qualities which go to make up
greatness of character—these were his. He
was always young. To that scoffer who, sneer-
ing at Lamb's habits, said that no man ought
to be a Bohemian after the age of thirty, as to
all the scoffers since, there is only the one old
answer—Lamb never got to be thirty.

"Of all men of genius I ever knew," said
Crabb Robinson—and he knew all that were
going in his day !— " Charles Lamb was the one
most intensely and universally to be loved."
Among them all, he alone was known by his
first name ; just as, at school, he had been, as
he always best liked to be, " Charles " to the
other boys : "so Christians should call one
another," he used to say. Reason revolts and
imagination cowers appalled before the forlorn
and hopeless conception of Wordsworth addressed as " Willie," or Coleridge as " Sam " !
For, you see, *this* man never posed, never
paraded himself, had no jealousy, nor petulance, nor pettiness. He never lied for effect,
nor harboured hypocrisies, big or little. He
was lucky in possessing that supreme antidote

to the pernicious poison of conceit—an abiding
sense of humour —"a genius in itself, and so
defends from the insanities," in Emerson's wise
words. Your solemn ass must needs take
himself seriously ; the man of deep, keen, quick
perception of the ludicrous can never do so.
When Coleridge, during a visit of the brother
and sister to him at Nether Stowey, addressed
to Lamb his maudlin lines, entitled " This
Lime-Tree Bower my Prison," in which he
gushes over " my gentle-hearted Charles," the
victim of these verses rebelled. " For God's
sake, don't make me ridiculous by terming
me gentle-hearted in print, *or do it in better
verse !* Substitute drunken dog, ragged-head,
seld-shaven, odd-eyed, stuttering, and any
other epithet which truly and properly belongs
to the gentleman in question."

" *Stat magni nominis umbra* " is Lucan's
stately phrase, to be aptly applied, in its best
and original sense, to almost every one of this
illustrious group. Yet, lofty as they loom in
the distance, far above our power as well as our
desire to belittle them, it may be not beyond
belief that too close and too constant contact

with some of them might have brought at the
last a certain satiety. It may even be breathed,
without irreverence and therefore without
offence, that we might have been just a bit
bored if allowed to listen without rest to
Coleridge, with his rhetorical preachments and
his melancholy, both born of rheumatism, rum,
and opium; or to Hazlitt, with his ingrained
selfishness, his petulance, his tea-inspired tur-
gidity; or to Wordsworth, solemnly weighted
with the colossal conviction of his own mission,
and tireless in his tenacity to attest the truth
thereof to all listeners. These, and all those
lesser ones, seem to me petty and tiresome
beside this spare, silent, stammering little
fellow, who loved them all and laughed at them
all; who gave them fitting reverence, and yet,
with affectionate adroitness, found fun in their
foibles !

How direct and delicate was his gibe when
Coleridge had been longer even than usual in
his endless endeavours to spin serviceable
ropes with his metaphysical sands: " Oh, you
mustn't mind what Coleridge says; he's *so* full
of his fun." I can see his twinkling eyes—

5

those wonderfully sparkling eyes—as he answered Coleridge's question, " Charles, did you
ever hear me preach?" " I never heard you do
anything else!" Coleridge was, indeed, quite
capable, in Hazlitt's sarcastic phrase, of taking
up the deep pauses of conversation between
seraphs and cardinals; and could have argued
—with the same ready confidence with which,
according to mocking Sydney Smith, Lord
John Russell would have assumed command,
at half an hour's notice, of the channel fleet
—on either side of the theses sent him by
Lamb just before he went to Germany.
These questions—" to be defended or op-
pugned (or both) at Leipsic or Göttingen," by
Coleridge are deliciously sly and sharp in
their stab at the complacent superiority over
lesser gifted mortals felt and shown by that
" archangel a little damaged." I can hear the
falsetto tone of his moralities growing shriller
before these two questions, especially, among
the others: " Whether God loves a lying
angel better than a true man?" " Whether
the higher order of seraphim illuminati ever
sneer?"

How deftly he punctured Wordsworth's sublime conceit, on his hinting that other poets
might have equalled Shakespeare if they cared.
" Oh, here's Wordsworth says he could have
written ' Hamlet ' *if he'd had the mind.* It is
clear that nothing is wanting but the mind!"
Even the Infallible One not only tolerated, but
valued, the acute criticisms with which Lamb
leavened his discerning praise of all his friends'
work; but when he, with kindly frankness,
rated a little lower than did their author the
" Lyrical Ballads," that author got into quite
a state of mind. He "wrote four sweating
pages" to inspire Lamb with a "greater range
of sensibility ; " and the tormented critic bursts
out : " After one's been reading Shakespeare for
twenty of the best years of one's life, to have
a fellow start up and prate about some unknown
quality possessed by Shakespeare less than by
Milton and William Wordsworth ! . . . What
am I to do with such people ? I shall certainly
write 'em a very merry letter." I wish that
letter had been saved for our delectation.

Then there was Manning, with his slight
sense of humour, and to him -then in China,

to his friend's loss — Lamb loved to write the
maddest inventions, and let loose his wildest
whims about their friends. To Coventry Patmore, on his way to Paris, he wrote, in an
amazing letter: " If you go through Boulogne,
inquire if old Godfrey is living, and how he
got home from the Crusades. He must be a
very old man now."

Good, honest barrister Martin Burney—of the
" If dirt were trumps " story—gave infinite fun
to Lamb by his oddities. Once he read aloud,
in their rooms, the whole Gospel of St. John,
because biblical quotations are very emphatic
in a court of justice. At another time he insisted on carving the fowl—and did it most ill-
favouredly—because it was indispensable for a
barrister to do all such things well. " Those
little things were of more consequence than we
thought ! " Burney quite approved of Shakespeare, " because he was so much of a gentleman;" and he said and did so many queer things
that Lamb wrote : " Why does not his guardian
angel look to him ? He deserves one; *maybe
he has tired him out !* "

It was George Dyer, above all, in whom

Lamb revelled, and who was meat and drink to him. Dyer was the son of a Wapping watchman and butcher, had been a charity-school boy at Christ's, and had become a publisher's harmless drudge. He was a true bookworm, eating his way through thick tomes, but digesting little. He seemed to find all the nourishment he needed in the husks of knowledge, while Lamb, in radical contrast, bit to the kernel with his incisive teeth. As to Dyer's heart, however, his friend was sure that God never put a kinder into the flesh of man; and his was a simple, unsuspecting soul. He was so absent-minded that he would sometimes empty his snuff-box into his teapot, when making tea for his guests; and so near-sighted that he once walked placidly into the river, as I shall hereafter relate. He used to keep his "neat library" in the seat of his easy-chair. Mary Lamb and Mrs. Hazlitt, going to his chambers one day in his absence, "tidied-up" the rooms and sewed fast that out-of-repair easy-chair, with his books within it: whereat, to use his own violent language, he was greatly disconcerted!

Lamb gives a ludicrous description of his
visit to these same chambers in Clifford's Inn,
where he found Dyer, " in *mid-winter,* wearing
nankeen pantaloons four times too big for him,
which the said heathen did pertinaciously
affirm to be new. These were absolutely ingrained with the accumulated dirt of ages, but
he affirmed 'em to be clean. He was going to
visit a lady who was nice about those things,
and that's the reason he wore nankeen that
day!" It was to this credulous creature that
Lamb confided that the secret author of
" Waverley " was Lord Castlereagh! And once
he sent the guileless one to Primrose Hill at
sunrise, to see the Persian Ambassador perform
his orisons! No one but Dyer could have said
that the assassin of the Ratcliffe Highway—
painted so luridly by De Quincey in his
"Three Memorable Murders"—"must have
been rather an eccentric character!"

Haydon, the painter, has told of one memorable evening in his own studio, when Lamb
was in marvellous vein, and met that immortal
Comptroller of Stamps who had begged to be
introduced to Wordsworth, and who insisted

on having the latter's opinion as to whether
Milton and Newton were not great geniuses.
Lamb took a candle and walked over to the
poor man, saying, "Sir, will you allow me to
look at your phrenological development?"
Haydon and Keats got him away, but he
persisted in bursting into the room, shouting,
"Do let me have another look at that gentleman's organs." Edgar Poe's Imp of the Per-
verse took entire possession of Lamb when
thrown with uncongenial men, and forced him
to give the impression of "something between
an imbecile, a brute, and a buffoon." Writing
of himself after the imaginary death of Elia,
he says, truly: "He never greatly cared for
the society of what are called good people. If
any of these were scandalized (and offences
were sure to arise) he could not help it."

No, nor did he try to help it, and we love
him all the more for this antic disposition he
was so fond of showing unshamed. And I
think that we need not grieve greatly because
his vagaries were not kept always "within the
limits of becoming mirth," when he had to deal
with prigs, pedants, or poseurs. Tom Moore,

tiptoe with toadyism, tried to look down on Lamb, doubtless feeling that he had accurately sounded the shoals of his shallow insincerity. The portentous Macready has left on record his unfavourable impression of the irreverent creature who stood in no awe of superior persons on pasteboard pedestals. That impression pains us no more than does the ungentle judgment of Thomas Carlyle. *He* found Lamb's talk to be but " a ghastly make-believe of wit," " contemptibly small;" and in all that was said and done he saw, from his own humane point of view, nothing but " diluted insanity." Curtly and cruelly he labelled this brother and sister, " two very sorry phenomena."

If our friend laughed at others, he was just as ready to laugh at himself; and his hissing his own play is historic. It is strange that, with his keen critical sense, he should have hoped for the success of this " Mr. H., A Farce in Two Acts;" produced at Drury Lane, in 1806, with the great Elliston in the title-rôle. Yet he had written to Manning in boyish glee: " All China shall ring with it—by and by." In the same

letter, he made fanciful designs for the orders
he was to give for admission, elate with antic-
ipation of the long run his piece was to have.
He sat on the opening night with Mary and
Crabb Robinson in the front of the pit (his
favourite place), and joined with the audience
in applauding his really witty prologue.   Then,
as the luckless farce fell flat and flatter, he
was louder than any of them in their hisses.
"Damn the word, I write it like kisses—how
different!" he growled, in grotesque wrath, in
his letter announcing the failure to Wordsworth.   Hazlitt, who was present, dreamed of
that dreadful damning every night for a month,
but Lamb only wrote to him: "I know you'll
be sorry, but never mind.   We are deter-
mined not to be cast down.   I am going to
leave off tobacco, and then we must thrive.
A smoky man must write smoky farces."   He
and Mary were "pretty stout" about it, but,
after all, they would rather have had success,
he had to own.   For he not only longed for
the fame, but he needed the money, which
that success in dramatic authorship would
have brought.

He delighted in playing all sorts of pranks
on his sister, and was quick to improve any
occasion to tease her. Such a scene is described by N. P. Willis, in his "Pencillings by
the Way;" where he relates his meeting and
making acquaintance with them, at a friend's
rooms in London. He and Lamb were chat-
ting, and Mary, not quite catching all their
words—she was then slightly deaf—asked,
"What are you saying of me, Charles?" In-
stantly he answered: "Mr. Willis admires *your*
'Confessions of a Drunkard' very much, and
I was saying that it was no merit of yours that
you understood that subject!" She took all
his freaks in good part, translating them in the
light of her affection for him, and of her fondness for his sweet and stingless banter.

His sense of fun bubbled up at most inapt
times. He had been asked once to stand as
godfather for a friend's child, and feared he
would disgrace himself at the very font. "I
was at Hazlitt's wedding and had like to have
been turned out several times during the ceremony. Anything awful makes me laugh; I
misbehaved once at a funeral." In all this

wayward whimsicality, one can detect that
same depth and intensity of feeling which
moved Abraham Lincoln to tell trivial stories
at the most solemn crises; which suggests a
sob beneath the maddest mirth of Sterne,
Molière, Cervantes; which drove Charles Lamb
to seize the kettle from the hob and hold it on
his sister's head-dress, like the clown in a pan-
tomime, to hide the breaking of his great heart
at the signs of the coming mania he had de-
tected in her. He accounted it an excellent
thing to play the buffoon sometimes, and was
willing to seem supremely silly, that he might
save his own sanity.

Acting conversely, this trembling sensibility
set the tears trickling down his cheeks, while he
was writing a playful paper; and made him even
"shed tears in the motley Strand, for fulness
of joy of so much life."

His largeness of soul was never shown in a
grander way than in his letter to, and his whole
conduct toward, Robert Southey, when the latter attacked, in the *Quarterly Review*, the first
collected "Essays of Elia"—"a book which
wants only a sounder religious feeling to be

as delightful as it is original." In the same
paper, he spoke arrogantly and offensively of
Leigh Hunt, his own political enemy, and
Lamb's most dear and most unjustly perse-
cuted friend. From so close a companion as
Southey had been, and one who knew him
so thoroughly, this hurt Lamb deeply, and he
wrote to Bernard Barton: "But I love and
respect Southey, and will not retort. I hate
his review and his being a reviewer." And in
the *London Magazine* he put forth the manly
"Letter of Elia to Robert Southey, Esq.;" of
which the latter said that "no resentful letter was ever written less offensively." Then
Southey—an exemplary if over-righteous mortal—sent Lamb a line of regret and affection,
and Lamb wrote generously back, and the mists
were melted away, and their friendship shone
more steadfastly than ever. Indeed, it seems
to me that Southey eclipsed Lamb in the spirit
he showed in this reconciliation, forasmuch
as he proved himself fine enough to forgive
the man whom he had outraged. We may
commend his conduct; "For right, too rigid,
hardens into wrong."

It is no part of my plan to dwell on Lamb's religious belief. Suffice it to say that it was, like that of most Unbelievers, too large to be labelled by a set of dogmas, too spacious to be packed within church or cathedral walls. It is a stale truism that credence, less than character, is the criterion of conviction; and all history shows that the doubters are, in nearly all cases, the most deeply devout. "He prayeth well who loveth well," Coleridge had learned; and it is my fancy that those lives, where love with voluntary humility waited on self-sacrifice, had taught him the immanent truth—"He prayeth *best*, who *loveth* best."

As to Lamb's utterances about these mighty matters, we may be sure that they took the tone of the man's utterances concerning *all* matters; and to them we may apply Hazlitt's phrase : "His jests scald like tears, and he probes a question with a play upon words." Or, as Haydon put it, "He stuttered out his quaintness in snatches, like the fool in 'Lear'."

IV

IN the midst of the vast Covent Garden prop-
erty of the Duke of Bedford is wedged a small
piece of alien land, on the corner of Bow and
Russell streets. It belongs to a certain Clayton
estate, and is covered by three houses, which
are worth more to us than all the potentialities
of marketable wealth hereabout. These three
houses formed but one building, at the time of
erection; which was late in the last or early in
the present century, as we may be convinced by
every architectural point of proof without and
within. It was built on the site of that famous
ancient structure whose upper floor was occupied by Will's Coffee-House; its cellars and
foundations still to be traced under the esti-
mable Ham and Beef Shop on that corner.
To-day, this popular establishment is thronged
for us, not with its actual eager buyers of cold
baked meats, but with the shades of Addison,
Swift, Smollett, Steele, Dryden, Cibber, Gay,

NO. 20 RUSSELL STREET, COVENT GARDEN.

Pepys, Johnson, revisiting their once favourite
foregathering place.

Of the three houses into which this block of
buildings has been divided, the corner house
remains entirely unaltered. Its neighbour, in
Bow Street—now a swarming tavern—has suffered somewhat at the hand of the modern re-
storer. It retains, on its upper floor, a small
barred cell, formerly set apart for some exclu-
sive or elusive prisoner from Bow Street station, just at hand.

The house which chiefly concerns us, No.
20 Russell Street, has been made higher by one
story, re-roofed, and re-faced with stucco; but
it has not been distinctly disfeatured.

Such as it was, it became the next home of
the Lambs, in 1817. At that time they had
lived for nine years in their chambers in Inner
Temple Lane, and it is strange that they
should have been willing to leave their beloved Temple, after having been born into it
again, and after having grown up in it again.
For Lamb's household gods planted a terrible
fixed foot, as he put it, and were not rooted
up without blood. " I thought we could never

have been torn up from the Temple," he
wrote; yet they did so tear themselves up,
and we are left to conjecture, for their reasons.
Mary told Dorothy Wordsworth that the
rooms had got dirty and out of repair, and
that the cares of living in chambers had
grown more irksome each year. More weighty
among their motives, no doubt, was the desire
to escape the incessant invasion of their privacy by welcome, and yet unwelcome, friends.
From this wear and tear they were not freed
by their flight, however.

In November, 1817, Lamb wrote to Dorothy
Wordsworth : "We are in the individual spot I
like best in all this great city. The theatres
with all their noises; Covent Garden, dearer to
me than any gardens of Alcinous, where we are
morally sure of the earliest peas and 'sparagus ;
Bow Street, where the thieves are examined,
within a few yards of us. Mary had not been
here four-and-twenty hours before she saw a
thief. She sits at the window working; and,
casually throwing out her eyes, she sees a
concourse of people coming this way, with a
constable to conduct the ceremony. These

little incidents agreeably diversify a female life."

Besides these novel sights, they found strange sounds in their new abode. A brazier's hammers were rankling all day long within, and by night without—but let Mary tell it, in her letter to Dorothy Wordsworth: " Here we are living at a brazier's shop, No. 20, in Russell Street, Covent Garden—a place all alive with noise and bustle; Drury Lane Theatre in sight from our front, and Covent Garden from our back windows. . . . The hubbub of the carriages returning from the play doesn't annoy me in the least—strange that it doesn't, for it is quite tremendous. I quite enjoy looking out of the window, and listening to the calling up of the carriages, and the squabbles of the coachmen and link-boys."

They squabble still of a foggy night—" a real London partic'ler"—and the noise is even greater now than it was then, and Covent Garden is filthier than ever, and the thieves go by escorted by a " bobby," and attended by a crowd; but the brazier no longer brazes,

and his discordant shop is now inoffensive
with noiseless fruits.

Here they lived until 1823, these six years
filled with increasing prosperity, with compara-
tive comfort, with happy friendships, with his
best work, with sudden fame.   His income had
slowly increased with each added year of
service in the East India House, and the earn-
ings of his literary work swelled it slightly.
That work had never yet received its recognition.   It was collected and published in two
handsome volumes in 1818, and the reading
world of that day suddenly awakened to see
in the obscure clerk, plodding daily to his desk
in Leadenhall Street, its most delicate humourist, its most acute critic, its most perfect essayist.   A little later, inspired by this success, he
set to work in these rooms in Russell Street
on his " Elia" papers, begun in the new *London
Magazine* for August, 1820.

So he outgrew his gloom and grew gayer,
although he was never for one hour out of the
shadow of Mary's constant imminent danger of
a relapse.   He drew around him many new
acquaintances, especially the theatrical folk of

this quarter, and more and more of the "friendly
harpies" he was fond of, on whom he spent his
time and squandered his strength. He needed
all he could save of time and strength for his
evening work on his Essays, after his day's
work at his desk. Yet he not only was not
allowed to attend to literary labour, but he
complained that he could not even write letters at home, because he was never alone; and
had to seize odd moments for all such writing at his office and from his work in East
India House. Stationery, too, he seized there;
and some of his unapproachable letters were
written on printed official forms concerning
"statements of the weights and amounts of
the following lots"! His task-masters there
would have gone out of their mercantile minds
could they have made accurate estimates of
the hard money value to be put by posterity
on those "following lots" which he thus un-
officially filled in!

Even there he was not unmolested, but was
constantly "called off to do the deposits on
cotton wool," he complained when writing to
Wordsworth. "But why do I relate this to

you, who want faculties to comprehend the
great mystery of deposits, of interest, of ware-
house rent, and of contingent fund?"

So his growing need and his growing want
to be alone were never gratified. " Except
my morning's walk to the office, which is like
treading on sands of gold for that reason, I am
never so—I cannot walk home from office but
some officious friend offers his unwelcome cour-
tesies to accompany me. All the morning I
am pestered—evening company I should always
like, had I any mornings, but I am saturated
with human faces (*divine*, forsooth) and voices
all the golden morning. . . . I am never
C. L., but always C. L. & Co. He who thought
it not good for man to be alone, preserve me
from the more prodigious monstrosity of being
never by myself." He could not even eat in
peace, for his familiars were with him putting
questions—presumably inopportune questions
—asking his opinions, and interrupting him in
every way. " Up I go, mutton on table, hun-
gry as a hunter, hope to forget my cares, and
bury them in the agreeable abstraction of mas-
tication. Knock at the door; in comes Mr.

Hazlitt, or Mr. Burney, or Morgan Demi Gor-
gon, or my brother, or somebody to prevent
my eating alone—a process absolutely necessary to my poor, wretched digestion. Oh, the
pleasure of eating alone!—eating my dinner
alone! let me think of it."

He did think of it, but to no practicable
remedial end; for, if he hated to have the in-
truders come, he hated still more to have them
go; and he had to avow, "God bless 'em!
I love some of 'em dearly!"

All this was a ceaseless drain on his vitality,
and a ceaseless strain on the nerves already so
overstrung. He wondered how "some people
keep their nerves so nicely balanced as they
do, or have they any? or are they made of
pack-thread? He" (I know not of whom he
spoke) "is proof against weather, ingratitude,
meat underdone, every weapon of fate." Lamb
was not proof against good friends, his sympathetic nature going out perpetually to them
to his own loss. Of Coleridge he said: "The
neighbourhood of such a man is as exciting as
the presence of fifty ordinary persons. . . .
If I lived with him, or with the author of 'The

Excursion,' I should in a very little time lose
my own identity." Only those of his susceptible temperament can comprehend this con-
fession, or his characteristic commendation of
John Rickman, Clerk of the House of Com-
mons, a newly made and highly valued friend :
" He understands you the first time. *You need
never twice speak to him.*"

Such were the tremulous nerves which
seemed to need the stimulus of alcohol, and
which were so easily swayed and upset by it.
The lachrymose and dolorous tones of Re-
spectability are forever croaking loud in lam-
entation that Lamb was a Drunkard. It is
not true. He was no drunkard. He could
not have been a drunkard with his delicate
organization. I believe that he suffered, un-
knowingly withal, from the malady now named
nervous dyspepsia; to which he was a victim, partly by inheritance, largely by his
own indiscretions. He was careless in his
habits, in his diet, in his exercise—walking
often at unfitting hours and for excessive
hours—and he had no regard at all for any
sort of proper precautions. Although habitu-

ally given to plain fare, and no gormandizer,
he was at times fond of outrageous dishes, and
fearless in his appalling experiments on his di-
gestive machinery. He audaciously claimed for
himself the stomach of Heliogabalus! Like
Thackeray, he had the courage of his gastro-
nomic convictions, and he has left an imperishable record of his love for roast pig, cow-heel,
and brawn. "I am no Quaker at my food—I
confess I am not indifferent to the kinds of it.
. . . I hate a man who swallows it, affect-
ing not to know what he is eating ; I suspect
his taste in higher matters. I shrink instinc-
tively from one who professes to like minced
veal "—admirable appreciation ! " C—— holds
that a man cannot have a pure mind who re-
fuses apple-dumplings—I am not sure but he is
right." And about a pig, just then roasting, he
wrote to Wordsworth : " How beautiful and
strong those buttered onions come to my
nose!" He could snatch a fearful joy even
from that baleful refection, cold brawn ; and
only at the thought thereof, as he is writing, he
glows with esurient unction. "'Tis, of all my
hobbies, the supreme in the eating way. . . .

It is like a picture of one of the old Italian masters; its gusto is of that hidden sort."

Conscientious in his cultivation of these admirably abnormal appetites ; fond of heavy, late suppers; addicted to too much tobacco; with friends forever to the fore to interest, stimulate, and thus unnerve him ; and with the unceasing terror that hung over their home and gave it its profound depression, it is small wonder that he found in alcohol just what he needed, and just what he should not have depended upon! He would tipple at times, and now and then he did get drunk, I do not deny: but never twice in the same house, as he truthfully assured a lady! That was a redeeming habit, surely. The fact, put in a word, is that he was affected by incredibly small quantities of stimulants, and as high as they pulled up his spirits, even so correspondingly low did his spirits sink afterward. His agonies of remorse, following a slight excess, were morbid, fantastic, never to be taken as true to the letter. After a trifling tipsy quarrel with Walter Wilson, he sent an apology, and added : " You knew well enough before that a very little liquor will cause a con-

siderable alteration in me." Mary wrote frequently : " He came home very *smoky and
drinky* last night ; " and then he would re-
proach himself the day after for " wasting and
teasing her life for five years past incessantly
with my cursed drinking and ways of going
on." His spasmodic efforts at reform were
born of these extravagant self-accusings, and
were equally needless and fruitless. " I am
afraid I must leave off drinking. I am a poor
creature, but I am leaving off gin." And he
did leave it off, with a moral certainty of his
abstinence lasting until his feeble stomach
clamoured for so much porter in its place that
Mary herself had to beg him " to live like himself once more."

His " Farewell to Tobacco " was more suc-
cessful, and more permanent ; it was not only
" his sweet enemy," but really his worst enemy.
" Liquor and company and wicked tobacco,
o' nights, have quite dis-pericraniated me, as
one may say ; " and of these three delights
wicked tobacco was to him the most delightful,
and withal the most dangerous. And so we
must not consider too curiously his famous

" Confessions of a Drunkard," with its terrible,
eloquent passage, beginning with this unfair
and unfounded introspection : " To be an object of compassion to friends, of derision to
foes; to be suspected by strangers, stared at
by fools." We are glad and proud to take him
as we find him—full of frailties, just as we
poorer mortals are ; it is not for us to sit in
judgment on him ; we say to the Philistines,
in Wordsworth's benignant words, " Love him
or leave him alone."

It was during the latter period of their residence in the Temple, and during their six years
in Russell Street, that Lamb produced the
greater part of the work he has left—small in
sum but great in achievement. It is not the
province of this study to dwell on his various
literary performances, but it comes within my
scope to speak of his sister's assistance in that
literary labour. In *all* matters he depended
greatly upon her. " She is older and wiser and
better than I, and all my wretched imperfec-
tions I cover to myself by resolutely thinking
on her goodness." During each frequent re-
currence of her pitiful craze—when she was

forced to be "from home," as he lovingly and
tenderly phrased it—he was lost and helpless.
"I miss a prop. All my strength is gone, and
I am like a fool, bereft of her co-operation. I
dare not think, lest I should think wrong, so
used am I to look up to her in the least as in
the biggest perplexity."

He did not overrate her. She was no com-
monplace creature, and she impressed all who
knew her well as a woman of fine judgment,
of noteworthy good sense, full of womanly
sympathies, sweet and serene. Hazlitt com-
mended her as the wisest and most rational
woman he had ever known. With strangers
she was unpretentious, mild of manner, reticent
rather than loquacious. In her bearing towards
her brother she was gentle and gracious always,
and she had a way of letting her eyes follow
him everywhere about the room, in company.
When looking directly at him she had often an
upward, pleading, peculiar regard. Mrs. Anne
Gilchrist, in her admirable monograph, has
called attention to the rare tact—excellent
thing in woman!—shown by Mary in dealing
with her brother's caprices and foibles, all

through his life. Indeed, there was absolute inspiration in her way of looking at, and acting upon, these matters. It seemed to her to be a vexatious kind of tyranny, which women use towards men, just because the women *have better judgment*—the italics are her own! She pours forth profuse strains of unpremeditated wisdom, in this same letter to Sarah Stoddart: " Let *men* alone, and at last we find they come around to the right way, which *we*, by a kind of intuition, perceive at once. But better, far better that we should let them often do wrong, than that they should have the torment of a monitor always at their elbows." Guided by such priceless principles, it is no wonder that she succeeded in never crossing that thin line which divides the domain of the judicious adviser, the opportune helper, from that of the untimely, incessant, ineffective Nagger. She once said, " Our love for each other has been the torment of our lives"—torment and assuagement together, as *we* know, and made sweet mainly by her simple sagacity.

Regarding her personal appearance, Barry Cornwall has told us that " her face was pale,

and somewhat square, very placid, with gray
intelligent eyes;" and De Quincey called her
"that Madonna-like lady." Her smile was as
winning as Charles's own, and when she spoke,
there came a slight catch in her soft voice, unconscious sisterly reflex of his stammer. She
was below the medium stature. strongly and
somewhat squarely built.

To this slight sketch of her looks and bearing may be added these, not too trivial fond
records, of her manner of dressing. Her gown
was usually plain, of black stuff or silk; but,
on festive occasions, she came out in a dove-
coloured silk, with a kerchief of snow-white
muslin folded across her bosom. She wore a
cap of the kind in fashion in her youth, its
border deeply frilled, and a bow on the top.

I cannot finish more fitly than with Barry
Cornwall's dainty touch, about her habit of
snuff-taking, in common with Charles: "She
had a small, white, delicately formed hand, and,
as it hovered above the tortoise-shell snuff-box,
the act seemed another link of association
between the brother and sister. as they sat over
their favourite books."

These favourite books were almost all the same, chiefly the Elizabethan dramatists, notably Shakespeare; but, unlike Charles—" narrative teases *me*," he owned—she was fond of modern romance and read many novels. " She must have a story—well, ill, or indifferently told—so there be life stirring in it," Elia wrote of Bridget, in his subtle portraiture of her in " Mackery End." Otherwise their intellectual tastes were in entire accord; and she was but a little behind him in having almost a tinge of genius in her keen critical faculty. She came naturally to a happy command of pure limpid English, which gave to her style the charm of her own personal flavour. This flavour was made the more racy by a delicate humour, exceptional in her sex.

These genuine literary qualities first had a chance to show themselves in the year 1806, while they were living in the Temple. Charles writes : " Mary is doing for Godwin's bookseller twenty of Shakspeare's plays, to be made into children's tales. . . . I have done ' Othello ' and ' Macbeth,' and mean to do all the tragedies. I think it will be popular

among the little people, besides money. It's
to bring in sixty guineas. Mary has done
them capitally, I think you'd think." And
again: " Mary is just stuck fast in 'All's Well
that Ends Well.' She complains of having to
set forth so many female characters in boy's
clothes. She begins to think Shakspeare
must have wanted—imagination!" And she,
too, has left a pretty picture of their common work: "You would like to see us, as we
often sit writing on one table (but not on
one cushion sitting), like Hermia and Helena,
in the 'Midsummer Night's Dream,' or, rather,
like an old literary Darby and Joan, I taking
snuff, and he groaning all the while, and saying
he can make nothing of it, which he always
says till he has finished, and then he finds
out he has made something of it."

She certainly had the more difficult task
in dealing with the comedies, and it was she
who wrote the greater part of the preface, an
admirable piece of musical English, ending thus:
". . . pretending to no other merit than
as faint and imperfect stamps of Shakespear's
matchless imagination, whose plays are strength-

eners of virtue, a withdrawing from all selfish
and mercenary thoughts, a lesson of all honourable thoughts and actions, to teach courtesy,
benignity, generosity, humanity." The little
book—" Tales from Shakespear, Designed for
the Use of Young Persons, Embellished with
Copper-plates," (by Mulready)—came out in
1807, and was such a sudden and assured success with older persons as well, that a second
edition was soon called for. Frequent editions
are still in demand. The new preface stated
that, though the tales had been meant for
children, " they were found adapted better for
an acceptable and improving present to young
ladies advancing to the state of womanhood."

She also did the larger share of " Mrs. Leicester's School "—a collection of charming tales
for children, over some of which Coleridge used
to gush, and Landor roar in admiration, in his
best Boythorn manner. A volume of " Poetry
for Children, by the Author of ' Mrs. Leicester's
School,' " was published later. After this her
literary productions consisted only of occa-
sional magazine articles, to one of which, " On
Needle-Work," I have already referred.

THE COTTAGE IN COLEBROOK ROW.

For the stories in prose, their authoress found the local scenery and colour in her memories of her youthful visits to Mackery End and to Blakesware. Indeed, the stories are supposed to be told to each other by the young ladies in a school at Amwell—the rural village which slopes up from the Lea and the New River, only one mile from Ware.

At intervals during these years, there had been short excursions out of town, longer country trips, and journeys to visit friends far from London. Charles had spent a fortnight at Nether Stowey with Coleridge, in the summer of 1797, and there had made the acquaintance of William Wordsworth and his sister Dorothy. She was, of all women he had known, Coleridge said, "the truest, most inevitable and, at the same time, the quickest and readiest in sympathy with either joy or sorrow, with laughter or with tears, with the realities of life, or the larger realities of the poets." She formed a warm friendship for Mary, and, like her, she had clouds come over her reason, though not till very late in life.

During another vacation, Lamb spent a few

7

days with Hazlitt in Wiltshire, and in other
summer holidays he visited Oxford and Cambridge.   He bore the country always very
bravely for the sake of the friends with whom
he was staying.

He had taken Mary to Margate in early years
—or, maybe, she took him, for she was then
twenty-six and he only fifteen—and he has told
us, in " The Old Margate Hoy," of this their
first seaside experience, and how many things
combined to make it the most agreeable holiday of his life.   Neither of them had ever seen
the sea, then, and had never been so long together alone and from home.   Many years after,
during his holidays, they went together again
to the seaside at Brighton and at Hastings.   In
1802, he was seized with a strong desire to go
to remote regions, and hurried Mary off for a
stay with Coleridge at the Lakes.   There they
passed three delightful weeks, although not in
the fairy-land which their first sunset made
them think they had come into.

Then they had a " dear, quiet, lazy, delicious
month " with the Hazlitts, at Winterslow, near
Salisbury, in 1809.   This visit, but not its pleas-

ure, they repeated in the following year; and journeyed from there to Oxford, Hazlitt accompanying them, and adding to their delight in the noble university town, and in the Blenheim pictures.

This trip, like most of their trips, was dearly paid for by Mary's illness. The fatigues, the changes, and the reaction after the excitement of society, disturbed her accustomed balance, nearly always; sometimes even before they reached home. So surely was this foreseen that she used to pack a strait waistcoat among her effects, on starting on any journey, however short. Her most distressing attack occurred on their way to Paris; a tour taken with needless rashness in the summer of 1822. She was seized with her mania in the diligence, not far from Amiens, and had to be left there in charge of the nurse, whom they had taken with them for just this emergency. It pleases us to learn that the friend who met and helped them there was an American, John Howard Payne. He escorted Mary to Paris, when she was fit to travel, two months later. There Crabb Robinson met them, and says: "Her only male

friend is a Mr. Payne, whom she praises ex-
ceedingly for his kindness and attention to
Charles. He is the author of 'Brutus,' and
has a good face."

In the following year, the Lambs were able
to make partial requital for Payne's good ser-
vices then, by helping him in his attempts to
produce his plays and adaptations on the
London and Paris boards.

With but a short holiday before him, and
friends awaiting him at Versailles, Charles had
gone on from Amiens as soon as he could be
spared; and had to leave Paris before Mary's
arrival. She found there a characteristic note
from him for her guidance. After pointing out
a few pictures in the Louvre for her scrutiny—
he had a pretty taste in painting as well as in
engraving—he told her: "You must walk all
along the borough side of the Seine, facing
the Tuileries. There is a mile and a half of
print-shops and book-stalls. If the latter were
but English! Then there is a place where
Paris people put all their dead people, and
bring them flowers and dolls and gingerbread
nuts and sonnets, and such trifles. And that

is all, I think, worth seeing as sights, except that the streets and shops of Paris are themselves the best sight." This was about all—these sights, the folios he loved, the fricasseed frogs he learned to love, and his meeting with Talma —that he brought away from Paris. Nor has he left any record of his visit, or of its impressions on him, such as we should have cherished.

V.

" WHEN you come Londonward you will find me no longer in Covent Garden; I have a cottage in Colebrook Row, Islington; a cottage, for it is detached; a white house with six good rooms; the New River (rather elderly by this time) runs (if a moderate walking pace can be so termed) close to the foot of the house; and behind is a spacious garden with vines (I assure you), pears, strawberries, parsnips, leeks, carrots, cabbages, to delight the heart of old Alcinous." Thus Lamb wrote on September 2, 1823, to Bernard Barton.

As early as in 1806, while living in Mitre Court Buildings, and anxious to finish his farce, Lamb had hired a room outside the Temple. Here he could work in quiet, free from his nocturnal visitors—knock-eternal, he called them, in one of his poorest puns. He had tried the same experiment in Russell Street, and when that refuge failed to secure privacy, he and

LAMB'S TWO HOUSES AT ENFIELD

Mary used to slip away for a few days at a time to furnished lodgings at Dalston.   But all these strategic devices brought only double discomfort, and they finally resolved to go away from town altogether.   Also they thought that they would like to have a whole house of their own, all to themselves.   Thus it came that the letter quoted above was written.   To that new home I now invite you to go with me.

As we turn from the City Road into Colebrook Row, we find an almost country road to-day, broad, tree-lined, a strip of grass running down its middle, and bordered by large, old-fashioned houses.   Beneath it flows that same New River to its reservoir near Sadler's Wells, hard by.   From the top of the hill we catch a glimpse on either hand of the Regent's Canal, as it comes out from the tunnel underneath; through the mouth of which wheezes and jangles laboriously the round-topped tug, with its chain of canal-boats.   It is a pleasant approach to " Elia "—as the present owner has re-christened No. 19 Colebrook Row—for the many pilgrims from all over the English-speaking world to whom it has become a shrine.

For these walls hold more memories of the brother and sister than do any of the spots we have yet seen. It stands nearly as when they lived in and left it, though no longer detached; a simple cottage of two stories and an attic, with stone steps mounting sideways. Its tiny front garden, flagged and flower-filled, is fenced off discreetly from the road, a Virginia creeper climbing over the railings.

The New River before it has been sodded over, and even the wool-gathering George Dyer, with his head in the clouds, could not tumble into it now. That was one of the most madly ludicrous scenes ever conceived, and was thus described by Lamb: " I do not know when I have experienced a stranger sensation than on seeing my old friend G. D., who had been paying me a morning visit, a few Sundays back, at my cottage at Islington, upon taking leave, instead of turning down the right-hand path, by which he had entered, with staff in hand and at noon-day, deliberately march right forwards into the midst of the stream that runs by us, and totally disappear." B. W. Procter (Barry Cornwall) happened to call soon after

and " met Miss Lamb in the passage, in a state
of great alarm—she was whimpering, and could
only utter, ' Poor Mr. Dyer! poor Mr. Dyer!'
in tremulous tones. I went upstairs aghast,
and found that the involuntary diver had
been placed in bed, and that Miss Lamb had
administered brandy and water as a well-estab-
lished preventive against cold. Dyer, unaccustomed to anything stronger than the ' crystal
spring,' was sitting upright in bed, perfectly
delirious. His hair had been rubbed up, and
stood up like so many needles of iron-gray.
He did not (like Falstaff) ' babble o' green
fields,' but of the ' watery Neptune.' ' I soon
found out where I was,' he cried to me, laugh-
ing : and then he went wandering on, his words
taking flight into regions where no one could
follow."

The " cheerful dining-room, all studded over,
and rough, with old books," is level with the
front garden, and unchanged except that its
several windows have now been cut into one
large one : as also has been done above, in the
" lightsome drawing-room, three windows, full
of choice prints." The prints and the old

books are gone, and rigid rows of decorous
volumes stare stonily from their shelves ; grim
horsehair chairs refuse the aforetime free and
unforced invitation; and the stuffed corpses
of dead birds, and other framed horrors of the
period all about, strike terror to our souls.
Against the wall, rears itself rigourously a prim
piano, from which *he* would have fled aghast ;
for, in her goodness, nature had given him no
taste for music, and he never had to pretend to
care for it.   He was constitutionally susceptible
of noises, and a carpenter's hammer, in a warm
summer noon, would fret him into more than
midsummer madness; but these single strokes
brought no such anguish to his ear as did the
" measured malice of music."   He affirmed that
he had been goaded to rush out from the Opera,
in sheer pain, seeking solace in street sounds !

However disfurnished may be this interior, its
tiny hall, its narrow stairway, its walls—on which
the Lambs may have put this very same queer
marbled paper—all are in the same state as then,
when they lived within and loved them.   The
most marked alteration has been in his once
" spacious garden "—around which he challenged

that professional jester, the obese, red-nosed Theodore Hook, to race him for a wager. That diminutive domain has dwindled now to an exiguous back yard, and a soda-water factory is built over its vines and vegetables.

Here the little household was enlarged and enlivened by the presence of Emma Isola, the orphaned grandchild of an Italian exile, who taught his own tongue in Cambridge, and who had been the Italian teacher of Gray and of Wordsworth. To her the Lambs, then visiting Cambridge, took a strong fancy; Mary especially pouring out on her the bounteous sympathy with which she flowed over for young people, and which won from all of them an equal fondness. They invited the lonely girl to visit them during her holidays, and finally they made her their adopted daughter, and their home her own. Mary helped her with French, Charles taught her Latin, that she might become a governess. Lamb was always quick to serve those who were poorer than himself, and, *giving greatly* all his life long, in Procter's words, he always had protégés and pensioners on his bounty. Yet he was curiously provident, and never lived beyond his simple income, never ran into debt. He could and did practise economy with himself, but he was incapable of parsimony in his dealings with others.

These are De Quincey's words about this side of the man : " Many liberal people I have known in this world . . . many munificent people, but never any one upon whom, for bounty, for indulgence and forgiveness, for charitable construction of doubtful or mixed actions, and for regal munificence, you might have thrown yourself with so absolute a reliance as upon this comparatively poor Charles Lamb."

But of all this the subject of this fervent, true tribute tells us no word. He prattled in print as freely and as frankly as Montaigne, though with none of the sentimental shame-lessness of Jean Jacques Rousseau ; and his delightful egotism has made plain to us his foibles and his follies. Yet, with all the rest of his life in evidence, we know nothing from *him* of

> " That best portion of a good man's life,
>   His little, nameless, unremembered **acts**
>   Of kindness and of love."

They had need, just then, of the brightness
of the young girl's presence, for they were
saddened—albeit needlessly so for all the comfort he had brought to them—by the death of
their brother John. Mary's illnesses were growing more frequent and more prolonged; and
Charles was chafing more and more under his
unending drudgery at the desk.   In 1822 he
had already written to Wordsworth : " I grow
ominously tired of official confinement. Thirty
years have I served the Philistines, and my
neck is not subdued to the yoke. You don't
know how wearisome it is to breathe the air of
four pent walls, without relief, day after day,
all the golden hours of the day between ten
and four, without ease or interposition." And
once he gave irate vent to a great outburst,
dear to all but to the shop-keeping soul: " Con-
fusion blast all mercantile transactions, all traf-
fic, exchange of commodities, intercourse between nations, all the consequent civilization,
and wealth, and amity, and links of society, and
getting rid of prejudices, and getting a knowledge of the face of the globe ; and rotting the
very firs of the forest that look so romantic

alive, and die into desks! Vale." And again:
" Oh, that I were kicked out of Leadenhall,
with every mark of indignity, and a competence
in my fob! The birds of the air would not be
so free as I should. How I would prance and
curvet it, and pick up cowslips and ramble
about purposeless as an idiot!"

It was in April, 1825, that his wish was
gratified, and his waiting brought to an end, in
this very Colebrook cottage. He had nerved
himself at length to offer his resignation to the
Directors of the East India Company, and
was surprised and delighted—having been kept
a few weeks in suspense—by the proposal
" that I should accept from the house, which
I had served so well, a pension for life to
the amount of two-thirds of my accustomed
salary—a magnificent offer. I do not know
what I answered between surprise and gratitude, but it was understood that I accepted
their proposal, and I was told that I was free
from that hour to leave their service. I stam-
mered out a bow, and at just ten minutes after
eight I went home—forever." To Wordsworth he wrote, on April 6, 1825: " I came

home FOREVER on Tuesday in last week. The
incomprehensibleness of my condition over-
whelmed me ; it was like passing from life into
eternity. Every year to be as long as three —
to have three times as much real time—time
that is my own –in it !"

He compared his sensations to those of
Leigh Hunt on being released from prison.
Indeed, the change proved to be too sudden
and too great for his happiness, and he yearned
for the "pestilential clerk-faces" which had so
long bored him : so one day, soon after, he
went back to the office, and sat amid " the old
desk companions, with whom I have had such
merry hours," and tried to feel really sorry
that he had left them in the lurch ! He has
told us of all his feelings, good and bad, at this
period, in "The Superannuated Man." He
could not quite thoroughly enjoy his freedom,
and was put to all sorts of devices to waste his
cherished time ! He re-hung his Titians, his
Da Vincis, his Hogarths, and his other beloved
prints. He marshalled his Chelsea China shep-
herds and shepherdesses in groups and singly
all about the rooms. He rearranged the ragged

veterans of his library; not longing overmuch
for the good leather that would comfortably
clothe his shivering folios. Few of them were
lettered on the back, and his reply to a silly
somebody, who asked how he knew them, was:
" How does a shepherd know his sheep?" It
was his fantastic humour that, the better a
book is the less it demands from binding!

Out of doors, he planted and pruned and
grafted; and got into a row with an irascible
old lady who owned the next garden. He sat
under his own vine and contemplated the
growth of vegetable nature. He explored his
new neighbourhood, hunted up ancient hostel-
ries, and made comparisons of their sundry and
divers taps. He prowled about Bartholomew
Fair, drinking in delight of its penny puppet-
shows, and its other " celebrated follies," as
they had been contumeliously called by sedate
John Evelyn, a visitor there nearly two cen-
turies earlier. He took long walks into the
country, with Tom Hood's erratic dog, Dash,
who imposed outrageously on Lamb's good-
nature; and went on excursions with Mary, farther afield—notably to Enfield, where they

made short stays with a Mrs. Leishman, into whose house they finally removed in 1827.

"I am settled for life, I hope, at Enfield. I have taken the prettiest compacted house I ever saw," he wrote. *No* health in Islington, was his complaint to Tom Hood; and yet, "'twas with some pains that we were evulsed from Colebrook. You may find some of our flesh sticking to the door-posts. To change habitations is to die to them, and in my time I have died seven deaths." He hoped for benefit to Mary from the quiet, and to himself from the change, and yet he looked forward to casual trips to town, mainly "to breathe the *fresher* air of the metropolis."

In those days they went to Enfield by coach twice a week or so, from one or another of the old inns, left standing to-day in Aldgate or Bishopsgate. No coaches run now, but it is a pleasant walk, up through the long northern suburb, still showing, spite of its being so citi-fied, traces of its old-time gentility in the square, stately, stolid brick mansions, the rural homes of rich city merchants a century since. We pass the High Cross at Tottenham, and

8

beside it the *Swan Inn*, descendant of that
Swan in front of which, within sight of their
beloved Lea, Anceps and Piscator rested " in a
sweet, shady arbour which nature herself has
woven with her own fine fingers:" but the
stream is polluted now, and the arbour has
gone, and Izaak Walton would not care for the
new *Swan*. So we pass by Bruce Castle, thus
named because it was owned by Robert Bruce,
father of the Scotch king—now a boys' school
—and come into that bit of road famous for
John Gilpin's ride, and so on into Edmonton.
Here we turn from the highway—by which the
stage-coaches kept on northward to Ware and
Hatfield—and going three miles farther, along
the cross road, we reach Enfield.

By rail it is ten miles from Liverpool Street
Station, and we whisk there in forty minutes
by many trains each day ; underground, behind
houses, over their roofs ; along by Bethnal
Green and Hackney Downs and London Fields
—where now can be seen no green nor downs
nor any fields—past Silver Street and Seven
Sisters and White Hart Lane, and many such
prettily named places; and last of all through

a stretch of real country into the dapper little station of Enfield.

"Enfield Chase" was a favourite hunting-ground of royalty until it was divided into parcels and sold after the execution of Charles I. Some of the old hunting-lodges still stand in gardens, one of them once tenanted by William Pitt. I have talked with aged men in the village who have seen, when they were boys, the "King's red deer" come into "The Chase" to drink from the New River: which winds through the land here, its waters drawn from the springs of Amwell and Chadwell, and from slopes with sunshine on them, and led later underground through pipes to supply London town. This *new* river was cut and engineered by Mr. Hugh Myddelton, citizen and goldsmith, who, "with his choice men of art and painful labourers set roundly to this business," in the year of grace 1609, and was knighted by the first James for his enterprise and success in his stupendous work. Tom Hood got out "Walton Redivivus, a New River Eclogue," and Lamb wrote a preface for it, in which he referred to his new home having the same

neighbour as his cottage at Colebrook. Doubtless he recalled, too, his out-of-town bathing-
excursions with the other boys at Christ's, and
how they would wanton like young dace in this
same stream. " My old New River has presented no extraordinary novelties lately. But
there Hope sits, day after day, speculating on
traditionary gudgeons. I think she hath taken
the fisheries. I now know the reason why our
forefathers were denominated the East and
West Angles."

We pass the town's old inns, with steep-
sloping roofs, and many a stately mansion set in
great gardens; among them the ancient manor-
house, renovated by Edward VI. for the residence of his sister, the Princess Elizabeth.
From here she wrote letters which you may see
in the British Museum; and in the Bodleian at
Oxford is the MS. translation, in her own hand,
of an Italian sermon preached here by Occhini.
This building—now The Palace School—contains one of her rooms, oak-panelled and richly
ceilinged; and in the grounds is a noble cedar
of Lebanon, planted in 1670. We look up at
the swinging signs of the *Rising Sun* and the

Crown and Horseshoes, past all of which
Lamb often went, and, doubtless, too often
did *not* get past without going in. It tickled
him to urge truly proper people to tipple
with him in these two taverns; and even
lady-like Miss Kelly—the actress with the
" divine, plain face "—and the austere Wordsworth were enticed to enter, and persuaded
to have "a pull at the pewter !"

And so, through a leafy lane bordered by
stately elms, with cosey cottages on either
hand, across a cheerful green, alongside the
rippling stream, we reach the " Manse," as
Lamb's home was called for many years—a
name it has only lately lost, when it was newly
stuccoed and painted. It has been rechristened
"The Poplars," from the four tall trees of
that species which rear themselves in its front
garden. In the garden behind, the old yew
and the bent apple-trees, and beyond the pleasant fields stretching away, are all as they were
when he looked through and over them to the
Epping Hills. The house has been enlarged
and changes have been made inside, and all is
hideously and shamelessly " smart."

Nothing in this interior speaks to us of its old tenants. They were seen, on their coming to take the house, by a schoolboy next door, who has given this pleasing description of them: "Leaning idly out of a window, I saw a group of three issuing from the 'gambogy-looking cottage' close at hand—a slim, middle-aged man in quaint, uncontemporary habiliments, a rather shapeless bundle of an old lady, in a bonnet like a mob-cap, and a young girl; while before them bounded a riotous dog [Hood's immortal 'Dash'], holding a board, with 'This House To Let' on it, in his jaws. Lamb was on his way back to the house-agent's, and that was his fashion of announcing that he had taken the premises."

In the summer of 1829, the family of three left this home, the care of which was wearing too heavily on Mary. "We have taken a fare-well of the pompous, troublesome trifle called housekeeping, and are settled down into poor boarders and lodgers, at next door, with an old couple, the Baucis and Baucida of dull Enfield. . . . Our providers are an honest pair, Dame Westwood and her husband; he, when

the light of prosperity shined on them, a mod-
erately thriving haberdasher within Bow Bells,
retired since with something under a competence . . . and has *one anecdote*, upon which,
and about £40 a year, he seems to have retired
in green old age." It was " forty-two inches
nearer town," Lamb wrote, and .it still is
there, next door to their first Enfield home,
as you see it in our cut: a comfortable cottage
set back from the road, vines clambering over
its small entrance-porch and hiding all the
walls. In its little back sitting-room were
written the " Last Essays of Elia." In this
house he remained for almost four years, and
in 1833 he made his last remove—except the
final one we all must make—to Edmonton.

VI

THESE years at Enfield were not happy years. They were both getting old; Mary's malady was growing on her, taking her more frequently *from home;* and even the visits of their child, Emma Isola—she was now a governess—mitigated his loneliness but slightly. His removal to the country had left his friends a long way behind, and, for all his urging, they could not come often so far afield for informal calls. "We see scarce anybody," he laments. Hazlitt and Hood and Hunt came occasionally; faithful Martin Burney fetched forth his newest whim for their amusement; and loyal Crabb Robinson often walked out to take tea or to play whist, or for a stroll in the fields with Charles. Once, as he has recorded in his "Diary," he brought the mighty Walter Savage Landor for a call: "We had scarcely an hour to chat with them, but it was enough to make both Landor and Worsley

express themselves delighted with the person
of Mary Lamb, and pleased with the conversation of Charles Lamb; though I thought him
by no means at his ease, and Miss Lamb was
quite silent. Nothing in the conversation recol-
lectable. Lamb gave Landor White's 'Falstaff's Letters.' Emma Isola just showed herself. Landor was pleased with her, and has
since written verses on her." Only this once
did Lamb and Landor come face to face.

Lamb had always hated the country. "Let
not the lying poets be believed, who entice
men from the cheerful streets," he querulously
complains; and he asks, "What have I gained
by health? Intolerable dulness. What by
early hours and moderate meals? A total
blank. . . . Let no native Londoner im-
agine that health and rest, innocent occu-
pation, interchange of converse sweet. and
recreative study, can make the country anything better than altogether odious and detest-
able. A garden was the primitive prison, till
man, with Promethean felicity and boldness,
luckily sinned himself out of it."

He was unable to read or write to any ex-

tent in hot weather; "what I can do, and do
over-do, is to walk; but deadly long are the
days, these summer all-day days, with but
a half-hour's candle-light, and no firelight."
Sometimes, of a "genial hot day," he would
do his twenty miles and over.   Once he took
charge of a little school during the master's
short absence; and his first exercise of author-
ity was to give the boys a holiday!   But
nothing abated his boredom, and even in his
bed he repined: "In dreams I am in Fleet
Street, but I wake and cry to sleep again."
And when he went to town, and sought in
Fleet Street fresh sights and fresher air, he
found no content: "The streets, the shops,
are left, but all old friends are gone.   .   .   .
Home have I none, and not a sympathizing
house to turn to in the great city."

He took lodgings for a while at No. 24
Southampton Buildings, within sight of his
former quarters at No. 34 of the same street
—a house in which Hazlitt frequently had
put up, not far from the house famed for his
"ancillary affection!"   The numbers remain
unchanged; and you may look at the queer old

NO. 34 SOUTHAMPTON BUILDINGS.

stuccoed front on any day you choose to turn
out from Chancery Lane. The house has a
strange, sloping roof of tiles, and altogether it
is quite unlike any of its neighbours.

But this impermanent residence in town
brought no real relief, for he found that the
bodies he cared for were in graves or dis-
persed. He sought solace in work, and made
extracts for Hone's *Table Book* from among
the two thousand old plays left by Garrick to
the British Museum. Hone had been grateful
to Lamb for having contributed already to his
Every Day Book; and had dedicated the issue
for 1826 to him and to Mary. In doing so,
he published his gratitude, most distastefully to
them, saying in his preface that he could not
forget " your and Miss Lamb's sympathy and
kindness when glooms outmastered me; and
that your pen spontaneously sparkled in the
book when my mind was in clouds and darkness.
These ' trifles,' as each of you would call them,
are benefits scored upon my heart."

Forgiving this fulsome gush, Lamb set his
pen to sparkling again in the following year,
and found relief in it. " It is a sort of office

work to me—hours ten to four, the same.   It does me good." The reading-room wherein he worked is now the print-room, a venerable and musty chamber, famous in those days for its fine specimens of the Pulex literarius, or Museum flea; and doubtless infested, too—for Lamb's irritation, as for Carlyle's, since the latter has left it on record—by that reader, still startling us there to-day, who blows his nose "like a Chaldean trumpet in the new moon;" and by that other, who slumbers peacefully with his head in a ponderous tome, and wakes suddenly, snorting.

The assistant-librarian of the Museum at that time was the Reverend Mr. Cary—" the Dante man"—a friend of the Lambs of recent years; and Charles found congenial companionship at his table, where he was frequently invited to dine.   Near the Museum, in Hart Street, F. S. Cary, the son of the librarian, had his studio; and there Charles would wander, on Thursdays, during the summer of 1834, and sit for his portrait, with Mary.   He is portrayed seated in a chair, and Mary stands behind him; the figures full length and half-life size.   This painting was never completed, and from it the artist made a copy of Charles alone, after death. Of this, Crabb Robinson said, a few years later: "In no one respect a likeness; thoroughly bad; complexion, figure, expression unlike. But for 'Elia' on a paper, I should not have thought it possible that it could have been meant for Charles Lamb."

Another portrait of him had been painted in 1805 by William Hazlitt; his last work with the brush, we are told by his grandson. This figure, in the costume of a Venetian senator, is well known in its engravings, and is considered an interesting presentation of the man. But, beyond the fine and forcible poise of the head—the noble head which resembled that of Bacon, said Leigh Hunt, except that it had less worldly vigour and more sensibility—this is to me an unpleasing picture. It robs Lamb of just that sensibility, and transforms him into a burly, truculent, ill-conditioned creature! He was thirty years old at the time this was painted. When he was twenty-three, an admirable drawing in chalk had been made by Hancock; a profile likeness, in which the superb sweep of the cranial arch and the subtle sweet lines about the mouth are most noticeable. This, the first portrait known of him, was engraved on steel for Cottle's "Early Recollections of Coleridge."

A striking piece of portraiture of his mature manhood has been found within a few years. It is a water-colour sketch by Mr. Joseph, A. R. A., and had been inserted, along with many other portraits, in a copy of Byron's "English Bards and Scotch Reviewers." This volume had been thus enlarged, in 1819, by Mr. William Evans, Lamb's desk-companion in the East India House, and he had doubtless induced Lamb to sit for this portrait with this intent. Another admirable likeness was painted in oil, in 1827, by Henry Meyer, and this was engraved for the quarto edition of Leigh Hunt's "Lord Byron and his Contemporaries," published by Colburn, in 1828.

The frontispiece of our volume is a reproduction of the portrait first engraved for Talfourd's "Letters," published in 1837. It is known as the Wageman portrait, engraved by Finden, and is perhaps the most noted and

THE MACLISE PORTRAIT.

the most attractive of any likeness we have.
Our Maclise portrait is made from an etching
done by Daniel Maclise, R. A., for *Fraser's
Magazine;* in which pages it appeared, as one
of "A Gallery of Illustrious Literary Characters," published from the year 1830 to 1838.
Of all the portraits of Lamb, however, it was
always held by those who had seen him that
Brook Pulham's etching on copper was the
most life-like in every way ever done. We are
fortunate in having so many portraits, some of
them so good; for Lamb never liked to sit,
regarding the desire to pose for a picture as
an avowal of personal vanity.

Of serious literary work, during this period,
Lamb did but little; his main pen product
being his letters to his many absent friends,
which give us such valuable and characteristic
glimpses into the man's lovable nature. He
wrote a series of short essays, with the title
" Popular Fallacies," for the *New Monthly Magazine* in 1828; and a little prose miscellany—
chat and souvenirs of the Royal Academy—
called " Peter's Net," for the *Englishman's
Magazine* in 1831. The year before, Moxon

had published a small volume of small poems
by Lamb—"Album Verses"—concerning which
a curious secret has only lately come to light.
The critics found little to praise in these verses
—and with good reason—and a review was sent
to the *Englishman's Magazine*, with a line to
Moxon from Lamb: "I have ingeniously con-
trived to review myself. Tell me if this will
do." He did not praise or puff his own work,
let me hasten to say; but his paper is rather a
protest against the errors and carelessness of
those same "indolent reviewers." Still, it is
a clear case of surreptitious self-reviewing, and
of it we may say, in the words of the coy
Quakeress—not Lamb's Islington Quakeress—
when she reluctantly consented to let her
ardent wooer enforce his threat to kiss her—
"it must not be made a practice of."

In 1833 appeared the "Last Essays of Elia,"
collected in one volume, from the *London*, the
Englishman's, and the *New Monthly Magazines*,
and the *Athenæum*. This work closed his literary life, not long before the closing of his
bodily life.

For the scene darkens swiftly now. "Mary

Received of Miss Mary Betham, Executrix to Mrs Anne Norman deceased, Twenty seven pounds, for my sister Mary Anne Lamb, being a Legacy and the said Mary Anne Lamb, being at present of unsound mind, not under my care

Chs Lamb

is ill again.   Her illnesses encroach yearly.
The last was three months, followed by two of
depression most dreadful.   I look back upon
her earlier attacks with longing.   Nice little
durations of six weeks or so, followed by complete restoration, shocking as they were to me,
then.   In short, half her life is dead to me, and
the other half is made anxious with fears and
lookings-forward to the next shock."   This was
in May, 1833, when he decided to remove to
Edmonton : "With such prospects it seemed
to me necessary that she should no longer live
with me, and be fluttered with continual removals; so I am come to live with her at a Mr.
Walden's and his wife, who take in patients,
and have arranged to lodge and board us only."

To lay a little more load on him, he lost
Emma Isola, one month later, in July, 1833, by
her marriage with Edward Moxon: their be-
trothal having been entered into "with my perfect approval and more than concurrence," he
writes.   In the same letter he says, as unsel-
fishly as always : "I am about to lose my only
walk companion, whose mirthful spirits were
the youth of our house."   He gave her, for a

marriage gift, his most cherished possession, a portrait of John Milton. Mary's reason was too clouded, at the time, to take interest in this affair, or even to understand it; but on the day of the wedding, being at table with them all, Mrs. Walden proposed the health of Mr. and Mrs. Moxon. The utterance of the unwonted name restored Mary to her composedness of mind, as if by an electrical stroke; she wrote afterward to the young couple: " I never felt so calm and quiet after a similar illness as I do now. I feel as if all tears were wiped from my eyes, and all care from my heart."

Amid all these added adversities, he tried, with his cheerful and cheering courage, to make the best of it all. He found compensation in that they were "emancipated from the Westwoods," and were settled " three or four miles nearer the great city, coaches half-price less, and going always, of which I will avail myself. I have few friends left there, but one or two most beloved. But London streets and faces cheer me inexpressibly, though not one known of the latter were remaining." And yet he struggled to town still more in-

THE WALDEN HOUSE AT EDMONTON.

frequently, and then only to find that, "with
all my native hankering after it, it is not what
it was. . . . The streets and shops entertaining as ever, else I feel as in a desert,
and get me home to my care." It is a touching sight, as we may picture it, that of the
lonely man, with worn face and wistful eyes,
wandering forlornly up and down his once
familiar streets, seeing so seldom any of the
once familiar faces. One day he met Mrs.
Shelley in the Strand, and was—she wrote to
Leigh Hunt—very entertaining and amiable,
though a little deaf. He asked her if they
made puns in Italy, and told her that Captain
Burney once made a pun in Otaheite, the first
that was ever made in that country. The
natives could not make out what he meant ;
but all at once they discovered the pun, and
danced round him in transports of joy !

During these lamentable days he saw his
sister but seldom : " Alas! I too often hear
her ! . . Her rambling chat is better to me
than the sense and sanity of this world." That
is to me the most tender and touching utterance
in all the letters since letters were invented.

At times, when her mind was not too turbid, she played piquet with him, and they talked of death ; which they did not fear, nor yet wish for. Neither had been ever quite able to say with Sir Thomas Browne, in Lamb's favourite " Religio Medici ": " I thank God I have not those strait ligaments, or narrow obligations to the world, as to dote on life, or be convulsed and tremble at the name of death."   Both wished that Mary should go first. Mrs. Cowden Clarke has told us how he said abruptly, one day—his blunt words covering his intense tenderness—" You must die first, Mary." And she replied, with her little quiet nod and kindly smile : " Yes, I must die first, Charles!"

Death was much in their thoughts during these days. Hazlitt had died in 1830, Lamb being with him at the last ; and in July, 1834, Coleridge ended, after long suffering, a life of " blighted utility," as he himself truly put it. The passing away of this dearest of the old familiar faces profoundly affected Lamb. " His great and dear spirit haunts me. I cannot think a thought, I cannot make a criticism on men or books, without an ineffectual turning

and reference to him." Nor did he linger long
alone. One day, in the winter of that year,
taking his customary walk, he stumbled, fell,
and bruised his face. The wound did not seem
serious, until erysipelas suddenly set in, and
rapidly drained him of his insufficient vitality.
So, on the 27th of December, 1834, the Fes-
tival of St. John and the Eve of the Inno-
cents, sank to sleep forever, in the fine words
of Archbishop Leighton, "this sweet diffu-
sive bountiful soul, desiring only to do good."
He was happy in not living, as he had said
long before, " after all the strength and beauty
of existence is gone, when all the ' life of life
is fled,' as poor Burns expresses it."

It was a peaceful and painless ending, yet
infinitely pitiful in its loneliness for one so
essentially social in his life ; his sister's mind
being too clouded to comprehend what was
passing, and his only two friends who happened
to be within reach—Talfourd and Crabb Robinson—arriving too late for his recognition.
They heard him murmuring, with his faint
voice, the names of his dear old companions.
Only a few days before he had shown to a

friend the mourning-ring left him by Coleridge, crying out, as he was wont to do, "Coleridge is dead." And it had been but two weeks since, when, during a walk, he had pointed out to his sister the spot in the churchyard where he would like to lie.

They laid him there, and she loved to walk to the grave of an evening, so long as she stayed in Edmonton. Indeed, she was with difficulty induced to go away for short visits to the Moxons and other friends. She was still at the Waldens in July, 1836, for an indenture has been shown to me lately, of that date and of that place, by which she disposes of the copyright of the "Tales from Shakespear" and of "Mrs. Leicester's School." This document was witnessed by Edward Moxon and Frederick Walden. Her signature to it is in distinct and unshaken characters, and her middle name is written without the final e, thus, curiously enough, spelling it Ann; for it was always elsewhere and by every one spelled Anne.

Later, her lucid intervals becoming less frequent and less prolonged, and her malady growing so nearly chronic that there was only "a twilight of consciousness in her," she was kept under care and restraint in St. John's Wood until her death, thirteen years after his. She rests by his side, in the same grave, as they both wished. His pension had been, with rare generosity, continued to her by the East India Company, and, in addition, she enjoyed the income of his small savings (£2,000) during her life; at her death it went to Emma Isola Moxon. This was the sum total of coin which he had gathered together; his real riches were lavishly dispensed during his life, and are hoarded now by all of us who love his memory.

We walk from Enfield by the same path across the fields through which Lamb escorted Wordsworth and his other visitors to the *Bell* at Edmonton, there to take a parting glass with them, before the return coach to town should come along. That famous inn is no longer as it was in his day, even then still in the same state as it was when Cowper laughed all night at the diverting history of John Gilpin, just heard from Lady Austen, and said that he "must needs turn it into a ballad when he got up," to relieve his reaction of melancholy. The balcony from which the thrifty wife gazed on Johnny's mad career is gone, the very walls are levelled, a vilely vulgar gin-palace rises in their place, and the ancient sign, bearing the legend, *The Bell and John Gilpin's Ride*, is now replaced by a great aggressive gilt emblem.

From here we turn, following Lamb's last footsteps, perchance none too steady, along the London Road, past the old wooden taverns, steep-roofed and dormer-windowed, set well back from the highway, and on the green in front a mighty horse-trough—relic of ancient coaching conveniences. The *Golden Fleece* and the *Horse and Groom* are all unchanged; in his odd irony the modern builder has left them untouched, because they have no historic memories! Then we wind around under the railway arch, and so through dull, straggling Church Street; passing the little shop in which—then a surgery—John Keats served his apprenticeship, and wrote his " Juvenile Poems; " and by the one-storied Charity School, " A structure of Hope, Founded in

EDMONTON CHURCH, FROM THE GRAVE OF CHARLES AND MARY LAMB.

Faith, on the basis of Charity, 1784," as
the legend reads over the head of the queer
little female figure in the niche. Its mistress,
drawn by Lamb's cheery voice as he came
out, used to run to her window to look at
the "spare, middle-sized man in pantaloons,"
as she described him.

For Bay Cottage—so called in his day, now
well re-named Lamb's Cottage, next to the
rampant lions on the gate-posts of Lion House
—stands nearly opposite the small school; and
it was through this long, narrow strip of front
garden, cut by a gravelled footpath, and railed
in by iron palings, that Charles Lamb walked
for the last time, and was carried to his final
resting-place. At its farther end squats the
small cottage, darkened and made more diminutive by the projecting houses on both sides.
On the left of the hall—large by contrast —is
their snug sitting-room, not more than twelve
feet square, low-ceilinged, deep-windowed, with
a great beam above. Mounting by a narrow,
winding, tiny staircase, with its Queen Anne
balustrade—under which partly lies the dingy
dining-room we find ourselves in his front

bedroom, his death-room, with one window only, as in the sitting-room beneath. Mary's large bedroom is behind, with two good windows, looking out on the long strip of back garden, wherein are aged trees and young vegetables. Nothing within these walls has suffered any change.

It is but two minutes' walk to the great, desolate graveyard, encircling all about the ancient church ; whose square, squat, battlemented tower shows its mellow tints through dark masses of ivy. Service was going on when I went for the first time to this spot, a few years since, and I waited until the officiating clergyman had finished his functions, that I might learn from him the location of the grave I had come so far to see. *He could not tell me !* He had heard that Charles Lamb was buried in his churchyard, but he had never seen the grave, nor had he been unduly inquisitive about it. After we had found it, a crippled impostor, lounging on the lookout for stray pence, scrambled up with affectation of mute sympathy, and swarmed down with scissors on the long grass about the small mound. That

parson's ignorance, the obscurity and desolation of the grave, the shocking structure of
the stone-mason order of architecture dominating it, well-cared for, and aggressively commem-
orating one " Gideon Rippon, of the Eagle
House, Edmonton, and of the Bank of England": all this is typical of the relation borne
by literature to Genteel Society in England.
Its combined cohorts of The Nobility, Clergy,
and Gentry do not know, and do not want to
know, about the burial-place of their only
Charles Lamb; but they do due reverence,
with naïve and unconscious vulgarity, to the
memory of the bank official who kept Books or
handled Money. Lamb himself, with his large
sense of the ludicrous and his small sense of
the decorous, would have been tickled by the
harmony between this state of affairs and
his whole life. To this grave—a peopled soli-
tude it is to us—come pilgrims from the other
side of the ocean, and sometimes the Blue-Coat
boys in small groups. The dreary and tasteless
head stone bears Cary's feeble lines, affectionate enough, no doubt ; but who cares to wade
through a deluge of doggerel, to learn that

Lamb's "meek and harmless mirth no more shall gladden our domestic hearth"? The acutest criticism on this epitaph was made by a knowing "navvy," who, having spelled it through painfully, said to his companion : " I'm blest if it isn't as good as any in the church-yard; *but a bit too long*, eh, mate?"

They have quite lately put up, in the church's single aisle, a mural monument, in which, under twin arches, perked up with crocketed commonplaces, are the medallion busts of Charles Lamb and William Cowper. Under the former—the only one which concerns us now—is cut this inscription, fitly followed by Wordsworth's impressive lines: "In Memory of Charles Lamb, the gentle Elia, and author of the Tales from Shakespeare. Born in the Inner Temple, 1775, educated at Christ's Hospital, Died at Bay Cottage, Edmonton, 1834, and buried beside his sister Mary in the adjoining churchyard—

> " ' At the centre of his being lodged
> A soul by resignation sanctified :
> Oh, he was good, if e'er a good man lived.' "

THE GRAVE OF CHARLES AND MARY ANNE LAMB AT EDMONTON.

INDEX.

BIBLIOGRAPHY,

BY

ERNEST D. NORTH.

The measurements given of the First Editions are for uncut copies, unless otherwise stated.

The edition of the Works and Letters of Lamb referred to is Canon Ainger's.

In giving the title-pages no attempt has been made to reproduce the various types used.

I. LEADING EVENTS IN LAMB'S LIFE.

1775.   Born February 10, Crown Office Row, Temple.
1782 (aged 7).   Enters Christ's Hospital School.
1789 (aged 14).   Leaves school and enters service of South Sea
                   House.
1792 (aged 17).   Enters service East India Company.
1795 (aged 20).   Resides at No. 7 Little Queen St., Holborn.
1796 (aged 21).   Publishes four Sonnets in volume of " Poems
                   by S. T. Coleridge."
1797 (aged 22).   Removes to No. 45 Chapel St., Pentonville.—
                   Contributes to " Poems by S. T. Coleridge,
                   Charles Lamb, and Charles Lloyd."
1800 (aged 25).   Writes Epilogue to Godwin's " Antonio."
1801 (aged 26).   Removes to No. 16 Mitre-Court Buildings,
                   Temple.
1802 (aged 27).   Publishes " John Woodvil."
1806 (aged 31).   Produces " Mr. H."—a Farce, at Drury Lane.
1807 (aged 32).   Publishes " Tales from Shakespear "—" Mrs.
                   Leicester's School."—Writes Prologue for
                   " Faulkener," by Godwin.
1808 (aged 33).   Publishes " Specimens of Dramatic Poets "—
                   " The Adventures of Ulysses."
1809 (aged 34).   Publishes " Poetry for Children."—Removes
                   to No. 4 Inner Temple Lane.—Lives at No.
                   34 Southampton Buildings.
1811 (aged 36).   Publishes " Prince Dorus."
1813 (aged 38).   Writes Prologue for Coleridge's " Remorse."
1817 (aged 42).   Removes to No. 20 Russell St., Covent Garden.
1818 (aged 43).   Publishes " Collected Works." 2 vols.
1820 (aged 45).   Contributes to the *London Magazine.*

1823 (aged 48). Removes to Colebrooke (Colnbrooke) Row, Islington.—Publishes "Essays of Elia," First Series.

1825 (aged 50). Retires from East India House.—Contributes numerous articles to Hone's *Every Day Book*.

1826 (aged 51). Removes to Enfield.

1827 (aged 52). Contributes Introduction to "The Garrick Plays," in Hone's *Table Book*.

1829 (aged 53). Lodges in Enfield.

1830 (aged 55). Publishes "Album Verses."—Contributes "De Foe's Works of Genius" to Wilson's "Memoirs of Daniel De Foe."

1831 (aged 56). Publishes "Satan in Search of a Wife."

1832 (aged 57). Removes to Bay Cottage, Edmonton.

1833 (aged 58). Publishes "Last Essays of Elia."—Contributes Epilogue to "The Wife," by J. Sheridan Knowles.

1834 (aged 59 years 10 months). Charles Lamb dies, December 27, at Edmonton.

II. FIRST EDITIONS.

[Arranged Chronologically.]

1796.

[1]

Title : POEMS | ON | VARIOUS SUBJECTS, | by S. T. COLERIDGE, | late of JESUS COLLEGE, Cambridge | [Quotation]. London : | Printed for G. G. and J. Robinsons, and | J. Cottle, Bookseller, Bristol. | 1796. 16mo.

Collation : Bastard Title, 1 page. Title. 1 page. pp. xvi. pp. 188. "Errata," 1 unnumbered page of Advertisement, "Published by the same author." Size 6¼ x 4.

Note. Coleridge says in the Preface, "The Effusions signed C. L. were written by Mr. Charles Lamb, of the India House independently of the signature their superior merit would have sufficiently distinguished them." There are four, viz.: VII. "To Mrs. Siddons." XI. Beginning "Was it some sweet device of faery land?" XII. Beginning "Methinks how dainty sweet it were, reclin'd." XIII. "Written at midnight, by the sea-side, after a voyage."

Price. Johnson Sale, N. Y., 1890, $9.50 [calf, gilt]. Sotheby's, 1887 [morocco, gilt top], £3 15s.

1797.

[2]

Title : POEMS, | BY | S. T. COLERIDGE | Second edition |, to which are now added | POEMS | BY CHARLES LAMB | and | Charles Lloyd | [Quotation]. Printed by N. Biggs. | for J. Cottle, Bristol, and Messrs. | Robinsons, London. | 1797. 16mo

Collation : Title, 1 page. pp. xx. pp. 278. Size 6⅛ x 4¼.

Note. Lamb's contribution was eight Sonnets and a Dedication, viz.: "Fragments," (6) "A Vision of Repentance," in Supplement, "Childhood," "Grandame," "The Sabbath Bells," "Fancy," "The Tomb of Douglas."

"There were inserted in my former Edition a few Sonnets of my Friend and Old Schoolfellow, Charles Lamb. He has now communicated to me a complete collection of all his Poems—*quæ qui non prorsus amet illum omnes et virtutes et veneres odore.*"

This volume contains two Prefaces, one to the First Edition, signed S. T. C., and one to Second Edition, signed "Stowey, May, 1797," S. T. C.

Price. Johnson Sale, N. Y., 1890 [calf, gilt top], $8.00. Sotheby's, 1887 [calf]. £1 18s. Sotheby's, 1888 [calf, gilt], £1 5s. Sotheby's, 1887 [calf], £1 10s.

1798.

[3]

Title : BLANK VERSE, | by | CHARLES LLOYD | AND CHARLES LAMB. | London : | Printed by T. Bens

ley, | for John and Arthur Arch, No 23, Grace- | church Street
| 1798.   12mo

Collation : Title, 1 page, Double Title, 1 page, Dedication,
1 page. pp. 95. Index, 1 page. Size 6⁵ x 4².

Price. Johnson Sale, N. Y., 1890 [morocco uncut, gilt top],
$28.00. Sotheby's, 1890 [original boards, uncut], £9.

1798.

[4]

Title : A TALE | of | ROSAMUND GRAY | and | OLD
BLIND MARGARET. | by CHARLES LAMB. |　Lon-
don, | Printed for Lee and Hurst, | No. 32, Pater-noster Row, |
1798. Small 8vo

Collation : Title, 1 page, Dedication, 1 page. pp. 134. Size
6⁵ x 4¹.

Note. Another edition was published the same year in Birmingham.
Printed for Thos. Pearson, pp. 134.

With the exception of the title-page this edition is identical with the
London one. Charles Lloyd's father lived in Birmingham, and it is sug-
gested that a few copies had been struck off there. [Dedication. "This
Tale is inscribed in friendship to Marmaduke Thompson, of Pembroke
Hall, Cambridge."]

Price. Dodd & Mead [morocco, gilt. Title in fac-simile],
$50.00. New York, 1885 [Full calf, by Bedford], $25.00.

1799.

[5]

Title : THE | ANNUAL ANTHOLOGY, | Volume I |
Bristol : Printed by Biggs and Co, For | T. N. Longman and
O. Rees, Paternoster-Row, | London | 1799. 16mo

Collation : Title, 1 page, Advertisement, 1 unnumbered leaf,
Contents, 4 unnumbered pages. pp. 300. Size 6² x 4¹.

Note. This volume was edited by Robert Southey, and published by
Joseph Cottle. Among the distinguished contributors were Coleridge,
Southey, Charles Lloyd, George Dyer, Mrs. Opie, Joseph Cottle, etc.,

etc. Lamb contributed "Living Without God in the World," pp. 90-92. A second series was published the next year [See Letter to Southey, November 28, 1798], which contained Coleridge's Poem "This Lime-Tree Bower my Prison, A Poem addressed to Charles Lamb of the India House," pp. 140-144.

Price. Sotheby's, 1885 [original boards, uncut], £1. [calf] £1 5s.

1800.

[6]

Title : ANTONIO: | A TRAGEDY | in Five Acts | by WILLIAM GODWIN | , London : Printed by Wilks and Taylor, Chancery Lane | For G. G. and J. Robinsons, Paternoster Row | 1800. 8vo

Collation : Title, 1 page, Advertisement, 1 page. (Dramatis Personæ, reverse) pp. 73. Size 8½ x 5

Note. Lamb wrote the Epilogue to this tragedy, which was produced on December 13, 1800, at Drury Lane. It was a complete failure. [See Letter of Lamb to Manning, December 16, 1800.]

Price. $3.50.

1802.

[7]

Title : JOHN WOODVIL, | a TRAGEDY | by | C. LAMB. | to which are added, | Fragments of Burton, | the author of | The Anatomy of Melancholy. | London : | Printed by T. Plummer, Seething-Lane : | For G. and J. Robinson, Paternoster-Row | 1802. 16mo

Collation : Title, 1 page, Dramatis Personæ, 1 page. pp. 128. Size 6½ x 4½.

Note. Lamb had written this three years earlier than date of publication, and had showed it to Southey and Coleridge, who tried to dissuade him from publishing it. It was offered to John Kemble in 1799, but declined. The original title for the play was "Pride's Cure."

Price. Johnson Sale, N. Y., 1890 [calf, gilt top, uncut], $19.00. Scribner & Welford, 1889 [boards, uncut], $30.00. Dodd & Mead [half morocco, yellow edges], $25.00. Sotheby's,

1889 [autograph from author], £11 15s. Pearson, 1889 [uncut, original boards], £5 10s.

1809.

[8]

Title: MRS. LEICESTER'S SCHOOL. | or. | The History | of | several Young Ladies, | related by themselves. |
London : | Printed for M. J. Godwin, at the Juvenile | Library, No. 41, Skinner Street | 1809. 16mo

Collation: Frontispiece, 1 page, Title, 1 page, Contents, 1
unnumbered page. pp. viii. pp. 178. Advertisement on reverse of last page.

Note. Lamb wrote for this volume "The Witch Aunt," "First
Going to Church," "The Sea Voyage." The other tales were by Mary.
The copyright for this and "Tales from Shakespear" was sold to
Baldwin and Cradock on July 21. 1836, by Mary Ann Lamb, for £15.
The original holder, according to the Indenture, was William Godwin.

Price. The Second Edition, 1809, fetched at Sotheby's, 1883
[original boards], £16 10s. [No quotation found on the First
Edition.]

1807.

[9]

Title: FAULKENER : | A | TRAGEDY. | as it is performed | at | the THEATRE ROYAL. DRURY LANE |
By WILLIAM GODWIN | London : | Printed for Richard
Phillips, 6, Bridge-Street. | Black-Friars, | By Richard Taylor
and Co, Shoe Lane, | 1807. 8vo

Collation: Title, 1 page, Preface, 1 page, Prologue, 1 page
Dramatis Personæ. 1 page. pp. 80. Size 8½ x 5.

Note. The Prologue was by Charles Lamb. The tragedy was produced at Drury Lane, December 16, 1807. The subject was taken from
an incident in De Foe's "Roxana."

Price. Spencer, 1890 [half morocco], £2 5s.

1807.

[10]

Title : TALES | FROM | SHAKESPEAR. | Designed | for the use of young Persons. | by CHARLES LAMB. | Embellished with Copper-Plates | In two volumes. | Vol I | (Vol II) | London : | Printed by Thomas Hodgkins, at the Juvenile Li- | brary, Hanway-Street (opposite Soho-Square). | Oxford-Street ; and to be had of all | Booksellers | . 1807. | 2 vols 12mo. Size 6½ x 4.

Collation : Vol I. Frontispiece, 1 page, Title, 1 page. pp. ix. Contents, 1 page, 1 unnumbered page. pp. 235. 10 illustrations. Vol. II. Frontispiece, 1 page, Title, 1 page, Contents, 1 page, 1 unnumbered page. pp. 261. 3 pages of advertisements. 'Colophon: Printed by T. Davison, Whitefriars.

Note. The greater number of these Tales are written by Mary, viz.: " Tempest," " As You Like It," " Winter's Tale," " Midsummer Night," " Much Ado." " Two Gentlemen of Verona." " Cymbeline," " All's Well that Ends Well." " Pericles," " Taming of Shrew," " Comedy of Errors," " Measure for Measure," " Twelfth Night ;" the others by Charles Lamb : viz., " Othello," " Merchant of Venice," " Macbeth," " King Lear," " Romeo and Juliet." " Hamlet." " Timon of Athens." These volumes seem to have been issued in sheep. there being no copies in original boards known. Each volume has ten illustrations, engraved by William Blake, from the designs of Mulready.

Price. Spencer Catalogue, 1890, in the original calf, £22. Dodd & Mead, 1886 [morocco, gilt top], $75. W. E. Benjamin, 1887 [morocco, gilt], $50.00. Sotheby's, 1888 [morocco, gilt edge], £10. Pickering & Chatto [original calf], £14 14s.

1808.

[11]

Title : THE | ADVENTURES | of | ULYSSES | by | CHARLES LAMB | London : | Printed by T. Davison, Whitefriars | for the Juvenile Library, No. 41 Skinner- | Street, Snow Hill | 1808   16mo

Collation : Engraved Frontispiece, 1 page, Vignette Title

1 page, Title, 1 page. pp. vi. pp. 203. Advertisement on reverse of page 203. Size 6⅛ x 4⅛.

Note. "I have done two books since the failure of my farce: they will both be out this summer. The one is a juvenile book—the ' Adventures of Ulysses,' intended to be an introduction to the reading of Telemachus! It is done out of the Odyssey, not from the Greek (I would not mislead you) nor yet from Pope's Odyssey, but from an older translation of one Chapman." See Letter to Manning, February 26, 1808.

Price. Johnson Sale, New York, 1890 [morocco, gilt], $20. Sotheby's, 1888 [calf], £3 7s. 6d.—uncut original boards, £3 3s. Sotheby's, 1889 [calf], £5 12s. 6d. Robson & Kerslake, 1889 [calf, gilt], £8 8s. Sotheby's, 1889 [calf], £2 6s. J. Pearson [calf, by Bedford], £6 6s. Scribner & Welford [original boards, uncut], $16.00.

1808.

[12]

Title : SPECIMENS | of | ENGLISH DRAMATIC POETS, | who lived | about the time of SHAKESPEARE : | with Notes. | By Charles Lamb. | London: | Printed for Longman, Hurst, Rees, and Orme, | Paternoster-Row. | 1808, small 8vo

Collation : Bastard Title, 1 page, Title, 1 page. pp. xii. pp. 484. Size 5 x 7¾.

Note. "It is done out of the old Plays at the Museum and out of Dodsley's Collection, etc. It is to have Notes." [See Letter to Manning, February 26, 1808.]

Price. Johnson Sale, N. Y., 1890 [morocco, gilt], $7.00. Sotheran, 1890 [uncut], £2 2s. J. Pearson, 1890 [half calf, gilt top, uncut], £3 15s. Scribner & Welford [boards, uncut], $16.50.

1809.

[13]

Title : POETRY | for | CHILDREN | ENTIRELY ORIGINAL | By the Author of | " Mrs. Leicester's School " | In Two volumes | vol I | (vol II) | London : | Printed for M.

J. Godwin, At the Juvenile Library, No. 41, Skinner Street, | 1809. 2 vols 18mo

Collation : Vol. I. Frontispiece, 1 page, Title, 1 page, 1 blank page, Table of Contents 2 pages. pp. 103. 1 page of Advertisement. Colophon : Mercier and Shervet, Printers, No. 32, Little Bartholomew Close, London. Vol. II. Frontispiece, 1 page, Title, 1 page, 1 blank page, Table of Contents, 1 page. pp. 104. Colophon : Printed by Mercier and Chervet, No. 32, Little Bartholomew Close, London. Bound in gray paper with green leather backs. Size 5½ x 3¾.

Note. Lamb contributed to this " The Three Friends," " To a River in which a Child was Drowned," " Queen Oriana's Dream," besides other poems not certainly identified ; the rest were by Mary. The Frontispiece to Vol. I. is a little boy seated in a Landscape, with the line " Keep on your own side, do Grey Pate. Page 20." Vol. II., the Frontispiece is " Penitent Richard standing in a Landscape," with three lines of poetry. At the time of the Locker Catalogue, 1886, only one perfect copy was known [see *Gentleman's Magazine*, July, 1877, for account of its discovery]. It was reprinted at Boston in 1812. A Mrs. Tween, daughter of Lamb's friend Mr. Randall Norris, has a copy of " Poetry for Children " given her by Mary Lamb.

Price. Sotheby's, 1888, £35 [Leycester's Sale, November 12-14].

1811.

[14]

Title : PRINCE DORUS : | or, | FLATTERY PUT OUT OF COUNTENANCE. | A Poetical Version of an Ancient Tale. | Illustrated with a series of Elegant Engravings. | London : | Printed for M. J. Godwin. | at the Juvenile Library, No 41 Skinner St ; | and to be had of all Booksellers and Toymen in the | United Kingdom. | 1811. 12mo

Collation : Frontispiece, 1 page, Title, 1 page. pp. 31. Illustrations : Frontispiece to face Title, " The Enchanted Cat ;" p. 6, " Minon Asleep ;" p. 7, " The Transformation ;" p. 10, " Prince Dorus and his Maids ;" p. 19, " Claribel Carried Off ;" p. 21, " Visit to the Beneficent Fairy ; " p. 23, " Prince Dorus Offended ;" p. 29, " Truth Brought

Home ;" p. 31, "Self Knowledge obtains its Reward." Size
5¼ x 4⅞.

Note. Only a few copies known to exist. The authenticity of this
volume is established by a reference in Crabb Robinson's Diary, May
15, 1811. There are two editions, plain and colored, not differing in
any other particular. The back cover should be preserved, as it contains a curious woodcut of Prince Dorus (The Long-nosed King) and
Aged Fairy. There are copies with Title-page put on cover within a
key border.

Price. Dodd & Mead [1888], $175 : colored [1888], mo-
rocco, $300. Sotheby's, 1883, £30. Sotheby's, 1889 [colored,
dated 1818], £45. Sotheby's, 1890, £29 10s. [original boards].

1811 ²⋅

[15]

Title: BEAUTY | AND | THE BEAST : | or | A ROUGH
OUTSIDE WITH A | GENTLE HEART | A Poetical version of an
Ancient Tale | Illustrated with a | Series of Elegant Engravings
| And Beauty's Song at Her Spinning Wheel | Set to Music
by Mr Whitaker | London : | Printed for M. J. Godwin, | At
the Juvenile Library, 41, Skinner Street ; | and to be had of all
Booksellers and Toymen | throughout the United Kingdom. |
Price 5s 6d coloured, or 3s. 6d. plain | Square 16mo, n.d.

Collation : Frontispiece, 1 page, Title, 1 page. pp. 32.
Colophon, London : Printed by B. M'Millan, | Bow Street,
Covent Garden | . Illustrations : Frontispiece, "Beauty in her
prosperous state." Face page 4, "Beauty in a State of Ad-
versity." Page 11, "The Rose Gather'd." Page 16,
"Beauty in the Enchanted Palace." Page 19, "Beauty
visits her Library." Page 21, "Beauty entertained with in-
visible music." Page 23, "The absence of Beauty Lamented."
Page 29, "The Enchantment Dissolved." Music : Beauty's
Song [music and second verse on reverse]. Size 5⅞ x 4½.

Note. The original is in paper-covered boards, roxburghe backs,
with woodcut, underneath which are written the words "'Go, be a
Beast!' Homer." The engravings are supposed to be by Maria Flax-
man, sister of the sculptor. On page 3 there is a water-mark dated 1810

Price. Sotheby's, July 9, 1889 [" Sale of Original Drawings to Martin Chuzzlewit "], etc., fetched £34. Sotheby's [plates misplaced], 1890, £20.

1813.

[16]

Title : REMORSE. | A TRAGEDY, | in FIVE ACTS. | By S. T. COLERIDGE | . [Quotation] London : | printed for W. Pople, 67, Chancery Lane. | 1813 | Price three shillings. | Svo.

Collation : Title, 1 page. | p. viii. Prologue, 1 unnumbered page, Dramatis Personæ, 1 unnumbered page. pp. 72. Size 5½ x 8¾.

Note. The Prologue was written by Lamb and spoken by Mr. Carr. The Play, written in 1797, was originally entitled "Osorio." It was brought out, revised, and re-named "Remorse," at Drury Lane, on January 23, 1813, and had a run of twenty nights. The London *Times* of January 25 said of the Prologue : "The Prologue was, we hope, by some 'd—d good natured friend,' who had an interest in injuring the play. It was abominable."

Price. Scribner & Welford [half calf], $6.50.

1814.

[17]

Title : SOME | ENQUIRIES | INTO | THE EFFECTS | of | FERMENTED LIQUORS. | By a Water Drinker. | London : | Printed for J. Johnson and Co. | St. Paul's Church yard | 1814. 8vo

Collation : Frontispiece, 1 page, Title, 1 page, Table of Contents, 1 page. pp. xxxii. pp. 363. Five illustrations, including Frontispiece. Size 3½ x 5½.

Note. Charles Lamb contributed sixteen pages to this volume anonymously, viz.; pp. 201-216, entitled "Confessions of a Drunkard." The author and compiler was Basil Montagu. The Essay, with a few additional pages, was reprinted in the *London Magazine,* August, 1822, and signed " Elia."

Price. Sotheby's, 1888 [calf gilt], £2 10s. Hitchman's, 1890 [boards, uncut], 21s. Sotheran's [calf, by Bedford], £3 10s.

Pearson's, 1889 [boards, uncut], £1 5s.   Scribner & Welford,
$25.00 [calf].

1818.

[18]

Title: THE | WORKS | OF | CHARLES LAMB. | In
TWO VOLUMES. | vol I | (vol II) | London : | Printed for C. and
J. Ollier. | Vere-street, Bond-street | 1818.   2 vols   16mo

Collation: Vol. I.   Title and Dedication.   pp. ix.   1 unnumbered page.   pp. 291.   Vol II   Title, 1 page, Contents.
1 page, 1 unnumbered page, Inscription, 1 unnumbered page.
pp. 259.   Advertisement, 2 pages.   Size 6⅜ x 4¼.

Note. The dedication is to Coleridge, and in it Lamb says : " My
friend Lloyd and myself came into our first battle (authorship is a sort of
warfare) under cover of the great Ajax."   There are two different issues
of this date, one on thicker paper and a trifle taller than the other.

Price. Sotheby's, 1887 [half calf], £1 5s. [calf, uncut], £2.
Sotheran [original boards, with book label of Wm. Hazlitt],
£5 5s. Sotheby's, 1889 [original boards], £2 10s.   J. Pearson,
1889 [original boards, uncut], £4 4s.   Scribner & Welford
[original boards, uncut], $25.00.

1823.

[19]

Title: ELIA. | Essays which have appeared under
that signature | in the | London Magazine. | London : |
Printed for Taylor and Hessey, | 93, Fleet Street, | and 13,
Waterloo Place. | 1823. 12mo

Collation : Bastard Title, 1 page, Title, 1 page, Contents, 2
unnumbered pages.   pp. 341.   Size 7¾ x 5.

Note. These Essays were contributed mainly to the *London Maga-
sine* between August, 1820, and October, 1822.

Price. Sotheby's, 1887 [calf], £1.   [Elia and Last Essays
together] Sotheby's, 1888 [russia, uncut], £11 15s.

1825-6.

[20]

Title : THE | EVERY-DAY BOOK : | or, the | GUIDE TO THE YEAR; | relating the | Popular Amusements, | Sports, Cere-monies, Manners, Customs, and Events, | incident to | the 365 Days | in past and present Times ; | being | A Series of 5000 Anecdotes and Facts ; | forming | a History of the Year, | A calendar of the Seasons, | and | a chronological Dictionary of the Almanac ; | with a variety of | important and diverting in-formation, | for daily use and Entertainment, | Compiled from authentic sources | by William Hone | [Quotation from Her-rick] | Illustrated by Numerous Engravings | London : | Printed for William Hone, 45, Ludgate Hill, | (to be published every Saturday, price Threepence,) | and sold by All booksellers in Town and Country. | 1825. 2 vols. 8vo.

Collation ; Vol. I. Title, 1 page, Double Title, 1 page, Ex-planatory Address, 1 page, Dedication, 1 unnumbered page. Preface, 1 unnumbered page, Illustration, " Bona Dea," 1 page. pp. 852. Vol. II. Frontispiece, 1 page, Title, 1 page, Dedi-cation, 1 page, Preface, 1 unnumbered page. pp. viii. pp. 832. General Index, 19 pages.

Note. This was issued in weekly parts and a new title-page printed when bound. The Dedication of the first volume is to Charles Lamb. To these volumes he contributed "The Months," April 16, 1826 [Vol. II.]; " Reminiscence of Sir Jeffrey Dunstan," June 22, 1826 [Vol. II.]; "Captain Starkey," July 21, 1825 [Vol. I.]; "The Ass," October 5, 1825 [Vol. I.]; " In Re Squirrels," October 17, 1825 [Vol. I.]; " Remarkable Correspondent," May 1, 1825 [Vol. I.]; "The Humble petition of an unfortunate Day," August 12, 1826 [Vol. I.]; "Quatrains to the Editor," July 9, 1825 [Vol. I.].

Price. Sotheby's, 1889, £2 8s.

1827.

[21]

Title : THE | TABLE BOOK ; | by WILLIAM HONE. | with Engravings. [Motto] Every Saturday. | London : | Pub-

lished for William Hone, | by Hunt and Clarke, York-Street
| Covent-Garden, | 1827, 8vo

Collation : Frontispiece [Petrarch's Inkstand], 1 page, Title,
1 page, Preface, 1 unnumbered page. pp. 870.

Note. This, like the other books of Hone, was issued in Parts, every
Saturday, commencing January 1, 1827, Lamb's contributions being, p.
451, "Mrs. Gilpin riding to Edmonton," and p. 387, "Gone or Going,"
and the Introductions to the Garrick plays, which are on pages 56, 67, 80,
96, 112, 128, 150, 162, 178, 192, 200, 224, 243, 256, 280, 291, 304, 320, 338, 352,
368, 394, 400, 417, 440, 443, 467, 480, 500, 514, 530, 547, 578, 595, 610, 642, 663,
676, 690, 704, 724, 737, 770, 784, 800, 817. In a note addressed to Hone,
dated January 27, 1827, written on the fly-leaf of a copy of "Specimens
of English Dramatic Poets," Lamb proposed this series, to which the
editor gladly acceded. The copy named is now owned in New York.

Price. £1 10s.

1830.

[22]

Title : MEMOIRS | of | THE LIFE AND TIMES |
of | DANIEL DE FOE : | containing | a review of his writings,
| and | his opinions upon a variety of important matters, civil
and | ecclesiastical. | By Walter Wilson, Esq. Of the Inner
Temple, | In Three volumes. | London : | Hurst, Chance, and
Co. | 1830. 3 vols 8vo

Collation : Vol. I. Bastard Title, 1 page, Frontispiece, 1
page, Title, 1 page, 1 unnumbered page. pp. lxii. Errata, 1
page. pp. 482.—Vol. II. Bastard Title, 1 page, Title, 1 page.
pp. xviii. Errata, 1 unnumbered page. pp. 527.—Vol. III. Bastard Title, 1 page, Title, 1 page. pp. xviii. Errata, 1 unnumbered page. pp. 685.

Note. On pages 428-9, Vol. III., appears Lamb's criticism on "De
Foe's Works of Genius." [Mr. Wilson says : "The following remarks
upon De Foe's Works of Genius are from the pen of the Author's highly
esteemed friend, Charles Lamb, and are original."] Pages 636, 7, 8, 9,
Lamb's remarks on "De Foe's Secondary Novels" appear. These are
of so characteristic a nature that they are well worth perusal. [Wilson
adds : "To recall the attention of the public to his other fictions, the present writer is happy to enrich his work with some original remarks upon
his Secondary Novels, by his early friend Charles Lamb, whose compe-

tency to form an accurate judgment upon the subject, no one will doubt who is acquainted with his genius."]

Price. Scribner & Welford [Full calf], $18.00.

1830.

[23]

Title : ALBUM VERSES, | WITH A FEW OTHERS, | by CHARLES LAMB, | [vignette] London : | Edward Moxon, 64, New Bond Street. | 1830 12mo

Collation : Title, Dedication, and Contents. pp. vii. pp. 150. Size 7⅜ x 4⅞.

Note. Dedication to Moxon. " Enfield, 1st June," 1830. This volume contains " Album Verses," " Miscellaneous," " Sonnets," " Commendatory Verses," " Acrostics." " Translations from the Latin of Vincent Bourne," " Pindaric ode to the Treadmill," " Epicedium," and " The Wife's Trial."

Price. Scribner & Welford [uncut, original boards], $15.00. Sotheby's, 1889 [calf], £1 5s. Sotheby's, 1890 [original boards], £1 10s.

1831.

[24]

Title : SATAN IN SEARCH OF A WIFE ; | with the Whole Process of | his COURTSHIP and MARRIAGE, | and who Danced at the Wedding. | by | an Eye Witness [Engraved Title] London : | Edward Moxon, 64 New Bond Street. | M.DCCC.XXXI.

Collation : Engraved (wood) Frontispiece, 1 page, Engraved (wood) Title, 1 page, Dedication, 1 unnumbered page. pp. 36. [Frontispiece and four illustrations.] Size 6¼ x 3¾.

Note. See " Letter to Moxon, October 24, 1831." Illustrations, [woodcuts,] should face pages 8, 21, 22, with tail piece [" To delicate bosoms, that have sighed over the ' Loves of the Angels,' this poem is with tenderest regard consecrated"]. The original cover should be preserved.

Price. Sotheby's, 1888 [calf, gilt edge], £2 3s. Sotheby's, 1890 [original wrappers], £8.

1833.

[25]

Title : THE WIFE : | A Tale of Mantua, | A Play, In Five Acts, | By | James Sheridan Knowles, | Author of " Virginius " " The Hunchback " &c | London : | Edward Moxon, Dover Street. | 1833. 8vo

Collation : Advertisement, 1 page, Title, 1. Dedication, 1 page, Preface, 1 page, Prologue, 1 page, Dramatis Personæ, 1 page. pp. 120. Size 8½ x 5.

Note. The Epilogue and Prologue were written by Charles Lamb and spoken by Miss Ellen Tree. Knowles, in the edition of his plays 1833, speaks of his debt to Lamb, etc.

Price. $2.50.

1833.

[26]

Title : THE LAST ESSAYS | of | ELIA. | Being | a sequel to Essays published under | that Name. | London ; | Edward Moxon, Dover Street. | 1833. | 12mo

Collation : Bastard Title, Title, Preface, Contents. pp. xii. pp. 1–283. Advertisements, 4 pages. Size 8 x 5.

Note. The Preface, somewhat changed, was originally published in the *London Magazine* and signed Phil-Elia.

Price. Johnson Sale, New York. 1890 [Full morocco, uncut, with First Series], $42.00. Sotheran, London, 1890 [Full calf], £5 10s. [Both Series, half morocco,] £2 10s. J. Pearson, 1890, Both Series [original boards, uncut], £10 10s. Scribner & Welford [morocco gilt on the rough], $60.00.

1796.

[27]

Title : ORIGINAL LETTERS, Etc. | of | SIR JOHN FALSTAFF | AND | HIS FRIENDS : | now first made public by a Gentleman, | a descendent of Dame Quickly, | from | genuine manuscripts | which have been in the possession | of the Quickly family | near four hundred years. | London : |

Printed for the author ; | and published by | Messrs. G. G. &
J. Robinsons, Paternoster-Row : | J. Debrett, Piccadilly : and
Murray and | Highley | No. 32, Fleet Street, | 1796 Small 8vo
   Collation : Frontispiece, 1 page, Title, 1 page. pp. xxiv. pp.
123. Size 6½ x 4.

   Note. Canon Ainger states [See page 404 "Elia"] that Southey
believed Lamb had a hand in this work. The Preface in particular bears
some traces of his peculiar vein. See also Letter from Gutch to Mr.
Bliss, page 155, Hazlitt's "Charles and Mary Lamb."

   Price. New York, 1886, [calf. gilt,] $15.00. Robson &
Kerslake [calf, uncut], £3 3s. 1883.

III. THE "ELIA" ESSAYS.

All Fools' Day . . . . April, 1821, *London Magazine.*
Amicus Redivivus . . . . Dec. 1823,   "   "
Bachelor's Complaint of the Be-
   haviour of Married People (A) Sept. 1822,   "   "
Barbara S—— . . . . April, 1825,   "   "
Barrenness of the Imaginative   Jan.
   Faculty in the Productions   Feb. } 1825, *Athenæum.*
   of Modern Art . . . .
Blakesmoor in H.——shire . . . Sept. 1824, *London Magazine.*
Captain Jackson . . . . Nov. 1824,   "   "
Chapter on Ears (A) . . . . March, 1821   "   "
Character of the Late Elia . . . . . Jan. 1823,   "   "
Child Angel : A Dream (The) . . June, 1823,   "   "
Christ's Hospital Five and
   Thirty Years Ago . . . . Nov. 1820,   "   "
Complaint of the Decay of Beg-
   gars in the Metropolis (A) . . . June, 1822,   "   "
Confessions of a Drunkard . . . . . Aug. 1822,   "   "
Convalescent (The) . . . . July, 1825,   "   "
Detached Thoughts on Books
   and Reading . . . . July, 1822,   "   "
Dissertation upon Roast Pig (A). Sept. 1822,   "   "
Distant Correspondents . . . . . . Mar. 1822,   "   "

Dream-Children ; A Reverie...Jan. 1822, *London Magazine.*
Ellistoniana ....Aug. 1831,*Englishman's Mag.*
Genteel Style in Writing (The) March, 1826,*New Monthly Mag.*
Grace before Meat...........Nov. 1821, *London Magazine.*
Imperfect Sympathies.........Aug. 1821,   "   "
Mackery End, in Hertfordshire. July, 1821,   "   "
Modern Gallantry ....Nov. 1822,   "   "
Mrs. Battle's Opinions on
   Whist....................Feb. 1821,   "   "
My First Play..............Dec. 1821,   "   "
My Relations ....June, 1821,   "   "
Newspapers Thirty-five Years
   Ago ....Oct. 1831,*Englishman's Mag.*
New Year's Eve.............Jan. 1821, *London Magazine.*
Old and the New Schoolmaster
   (The)..................May, 1821,   "   "
Old Benchers of the Inner Tem-
   ple (The)................Sept. 1821,   "   "
Old China..................March 1823,   "   "
Old Margate Hoy (The)......July, 1823,   "   "
On Some of the Old Actors....Feb. 1822,   "   "
On the Artificial Comedy of the
   Last Century ....April, 1822,   "   "
On the Acting of Munden.....Oct. 1822,   "   "
Oxford in the Vacation.......Oct. 1820,   "   "
Poor Relations..............May, 1823,   "   "
Popular Fallacies :   { Jan. to Sept. 1826, } *New Monthly Mag*

   1. That a Bully is always a Coward....   "   "
   2. That Ill-gotten Gain never prospers.   "   "
   3. That a man must not laugh at his
      own jest.....................   "   "
   4. That such a one shows his breeding,
      etc..........................   "   "
   5. That the Poor copy the vices of the
      Rich.........................   "   "

6. That Enough is as good as a Feast...*New Monthly Mag.*
7. Of two Disputants, the Warmest is generally in the Wrong.... ..... " "
8. That verbal Allusions are not Wit, because they will not bear translation .... " "
9. That the Worst Puns are the Best... " "
10. That Handsome is that Handsome Does ... . " "
11. That we must not look a Gift-Horse in the Mouth.................... " "
12. That Home is Home though it is never so Homely.............. " "
13. That you must love me and love My Dog .... " "
14. That we should rise with the Lark.. " "
15. That we should lie down with the Lamb........................ " "
16. That a sulky temper is a Misfortune. " "
Praise of Chimney-Sweepers(The)May, 1822, *London Magazine.*
Quakers' Meeting (A)........ April, 1821, " "
Rejoicings upon the New Year's Coming of Age............Jan. 1823. " "
Sanity of True Genius........May, 1826, *New Monthly Mag.*
Some Sonnets of Sir Philip Sydney..... ....Sept. 1823, *London Magazine.*
South-Sea House (The) ....Aug. 1820, " "
Stage Illusion...............Aug. 1825, " "
Superannuated Man (The).....
To the Shade of Elliston......Aug. 1831, *Englishman's Mag.*
Tombs in the Abbey (The) ....Oct. 1823, *London Magazine.*
Two Races of Men (The).....Dec. 1820. " "
Valentine's Day............Feb. 14, 1821, *The Indicator.*
Wedding (The)..............June, 1825, *London Magazine.*
Witches, and Other Night Fears.Oct. 1821, " "

IV. REVIEWS, POEMS, ESSAYS, Etc.

Annual Anthology (Cottle's), 1799, " Living without God in the World."

Athenæum (*The*), [Prose] February 11, 1832, " On the Death of Munden." January 12, 19, 26, February 2, 1833, " On the Total Defect of the Quality of Imagination observable in the works of Modern British Artists." November 30, 1833, " Thoughts on Presents of Game." January 4, May 31, June 7, July 19, 1834, " Table Talk by the Late Elia." [Poems] January 7, 1832, " The Self Enchanted." February 25, " The Parting Speech of the Celestial Messenger to the Poet." July 7, " Existence, considered in itself, no blessing." March 9, 1833, " Christian Names of Women." December 7, " To a friend on his Marriage." December 21, " To T. Stothard, Esq , on his Illustrations of the Poems of Mr. Rogers." February 15, 1834, " Cheap Gifts : A Sonnet." July 26, 1834, " To Clara N." March 14, 1835. ' To Margaret W."

Blackwood's Magazine, December, 1828, " The Wife's Trial." January, 1829, " The Gipsy's Malison." May, 1829, " The Christening."

Bristol Journal (*The*), Febru-

ary 7, 1819, " Miss Kelley at Bath." (Signed, * * * *)

Champion (*The*), December 4, 1814, " On the Melancholy of Tailors." (Signed, Burton Junior.)

Examiner (*The*), 1822, " Work." June 6, 1813, " The Reynolds Gallery," " Theatrical Notices." July 4, 1819, " Richard Brome's Jovial Crew," " Isaac Bickerstaff's Hypocrite," August 2, 1819, " New Pieces at the Lyceum," August, 1819. (These were all signed * * * *) January 16, 1820, " First Fruits of Australian Poetry," (numerous Epigrams, etc.)

Englishman's Magazine, September, 1831, " Recollections of a late Royal Academician."

Gentleman's Magazine (*The*), June, 1813, " Recollections of Christ's Hospital."

Gem (*The*), 1830, " Saturday Night."

Hone's Every Day Book, April 16, 1826, " The Months." June 22, 1826, " Reminiscence of Sir Jeffrey Dunstan." July 21, 1825, " Captain Starkey." October 5, 1825. " The Ass." October 17, 1825, " In Re Squirrels." May 1, 1825, " Remarkable Correspondent." August 12, 1825. " The Humble Petition of an Un-

fortunate Day." July 9,1825, " Quatrains to the Editor."
Hone's Table Book, p. 454 [1827]. " Mrs Gilpin riding to Edmonton." 1827. " Epicedium," " Gone or Going," p. 357.
Indicator (The), March 7, 1821, " Elia to his Correspondents."
London Magazine, April, 1821. " Leisure." December, 1822. " Guy Faux." October, 1823. " Letter to Robert Southey. Esq." October. 1823. " Letter of Elia to his Correspondents." November, 1823. " The Gentle Giantess." November, 1823. " On a Passage in the Tempest." January, 1825, " Letter to an Old Gentleman whose Education has been Neglected." January, 1825, " Biographical Memoirs of Mr. Liston." February, 1825, " Autobiography of Mr. Munden." March, 1825. " Reflections in the Pillory." April, 1825, " The Last Peach."
Morning Chronicle, 1794, Sonnet, commencing : " As when a child on some long winter's night." [Written probably in conjunction with Coleridge.]
Monthly Magazine, January, 1797, " To Sara and her Samuel."

New Monthly Magazine, 1825, " The Illustrious Defunct." 1826, " The Religion of Actors." June, 1826. " A Popular Fallacy." April, 1835. " Charles Lamb's Autobiography." 1835, " On the Death of Coleridge."
Quarterly Review, October, 1814, " Wordsworth's Excursion."
Reflector (The) [Leigh Hunt's], 1811, Vol. IV., " A Farewell to Tobacco."
Theatralia (No. 1). " On the Tragedies of Shakespeare." 1811. " Specimens from the writings of Fuller." 1811 (No. 4). " On the Genius and Character of Hogarth," 1811 (No. 3). " On Burial Societies, and the Character of an Under taker," 1811 (No. 2, Art. 15). " On the Inconveniences resulting from being hanged," 1811 (No. 3, Art. 13), " On the Danger of Confounding Moral with Personal Deformity." 1811 (No. 2, Art. 15). " Hospita on the Immoderate Indulgence of the Pleasures of the Palate," 1811 (No. 4). " Edax on Appetite," 1811 (No. 4). " On the Custom of Hissing at Theatres," 1811 (No 3, Art. 11). " The Good Clerk," 1811 (No. 4, Art. 23).

V. COLLECTED WORKS.

1813. The Works of Charles Lamb. In two volumes. London, C. & J. Ollier, 1818. 2 vols. 12mo.
The first collected edition.

1835. The Prose Works of Charles Lamb. London, Moxon, 1835. 3 vols. 12mo.

1836. Prose Works of Charles Lamb. London, Moxon. 1836. 3 vols. 8vo.

1838. The Prose Works of Charles Lamb. London, Moxon, 1838. 3 vols. 12mo.
—— The Same, 1839.
—— The Same. 4 vols. 1840.
—— Another edition, 1847.

1838. The Works of Charles Lamb, comprising his Letters, Poems, Essays of Elia, etc., etc., with Sketch of his Life, by T. N. Talfourd. New York, Harper & Bros., 1838. 2 vols. 12mo.

1840. The Works of Charles Lamb [edited by Talfourd, with Sketch of Life, portrait and engraved title]. London. Moxon, 1840. 8vo.
—— The Same. 1845. 8vo.
—— The Same. 1852. 8vo.

1850. The Prose and Poetical Works of Charles Lamb, with his Letters and Life. by T. N. Talfourd. London, Moxon. 1850. 4 vols. 12mo.
—— Another edition. London, 1852.
—— Another edition. London, 1855.

1855. Works, with a Sketch of his Life and Final Memorials, by Sir T. N. Talfourd. New York, Harper & Bros., 1855. 2 vols. 12mo.

1856. —— Another edition. Philadelphia, W. P. Hazard, 1856. 4 vols. 8vo.

1857. Works, with Life, by Sir T. N. Talfourd. New York, 1857. 2 vols. 12mo.

1859. The Works of Charles Lamb. A new edition. [Portrait by Wageman, engraved title of Christ's Hospital.] London, Moxon & Co., 1859. 8vo.

1865. The Works of Charles Lamb. A new edition. In five volumes. [Portrait by Wageman.] Boston, William Veazie, 1865. 5 vols. 12mo.
A large paper edition of only 100 copies was issued at the same time.

1865. The Works of Charles Lamb, corrected and revised, with Portrait. New York, Widdleton, 1865. 5 vols. 12mo.

1867. The Works of Charles Lamb, including his most interesting Letters, collected and edited, with Memorials, by Sir T. N. Talfourd. A new edition. London, Bell & Daldy, 1867. 8vo.

1868. The Complete Correspondence and Works of Charles Lamb, with an "Essay on the Genius of Charles

Lamb," by George Augustus Sala [edited by W. C. Hazlitt]. London, E. Moxon & Co., 1868. 4 vols. 12mo.

It is only justice to Mr. Hazlitt to say that this edition was issued without his name upon the title-page; he did not even see the proofs.

1870. The Complete Correspondence and Works of Charles Lamb, with an Essay on his Life and Genius, by Thomas Purnell, aided by the Recollections of the author's adopted daughter [Mrs. Moxon]. [Portrait of Charles and Mary, the former seated.] London, Edward Moxon, 1870. 4 vols. 12mo.

This edition contains a new Preface by Thomas Purnell. It has the first volume withdrawn of the issue of 1868.

1870. Works and Letters, by Talfourd. London, Bell & Daldy, 1870. 8vo.

1874. The Complete Works, in Prose and Verse, of Charles Lamb, from the original editions, with the cancelled passages restored, and many pieces now first collected. Edited and prefaced by R. H. Shepherd. [Portrait.] London, Chatto & Windus, 1874. 8vo.
——The Same, 1875.
——The Same, 1878.

1875. The Life, Letters, and Writings of Charles Lamb, edited, with Notes and Illustrations by Percy Fitzgerald. [Portrait by William Hazlitt.] London, Edward Moxon, 1875. 6 vols. 8vo.

In this edition the narrative por-

tion of Talfourd's two works has been retained, condensed into one continuous narrative, with additions both in text and notes, while the Letters are separated from Talfourd's original matter and arranged in groups, forty new ones being added.

——The Same, 1876.
——The Same, 1882-4.

1876. Works. Edited by Charles Kent. [Routledge's Standard Library.] London, 1876. Crown 8vo.
——The Same. London, 1889.

1876. Works, Poetical and Dramatic. Tales, etc. Routledge, 1876. 8vo.

1879. The Complete Works: with a Sketch of his Life, by Sir T. N. Talfourd. Personal Reminiscences of Lamb, Coleridge, Southey, Wordsworth, and J. Cottle, by an American Friend. [Enfield Edition.] Portrait and Engravings. Philadelphia, 1879. Amies Pub. Co. 8vo.

1880. Works, etc., new edition. [Standard.] New York, 1880. 3 vols. 12mo.

1884. Works, etc. New York, 1884. 5 vols. 12mo.

1886. The Life, Letters, and Writings of Charles Lamb. Edited, with Notes and Illustrations, by Percy Fitzgerald. London, John Slark, 1886. 6 vols. 12mo.

An exact reprint of the edition of 1875.

1888. [Collected edition. Edited, with Notes and Introductions, by Alfred Ainger.] Tales from Shakespeare, by Charles

172 Bibliography.

and Mary Lamb, 1878.—The Essays of Elia, 1883.—Poems, Plays, and Miscellaneous Essays, 1884.—Mrs. Leicester's School and other Writings in Prose and Verse, 1885.—The Letters of Charles Lamb, newly arranged, with additions.

Portrait. 2 vols. 1888.— Charles Lamb, 1888.

This is by far the best edition of Lamb's Works. Excepting the biography, the dates given are those of the first editions. The latter was published in the "English Men of Letters" Series, in 1878, but is slightly enlarged so as to be uniform.

VI. SINGLE WORKS.

[*Arranged Alphabetically.*]

1808. Adventures of Ulysses (The), by Charles Lamb. London, 1808. 12mo.
The First Edition.

1819. Adventures of Ulysses (The) [by C. L.]. A new edition. London, 1819. 12mo.

1827. Adventures of Ulysses [by C. L.]. Designed as a supplement to the Adventures of Telemachus. A new edition. Baldwin, Cradock & Joy, London, 1827. 12mo.

1839. Adventures of Ulysses (The) [by C. L.]. [Engraving.] London, 1839. 12mo.

1840.—— Another edition. To which are added Mrs. Leicester's School, etc. London, 1840. 8vo.

1845.—— Another edition. London, 1845. 12mo.

1848.—— Another edition. London, 1848. 12mo.

1879. Adventures of Ulysses [Half Hour Series]. N. Y., Harper & Bros., 1879. 32mo.

1886. Adventures of Ulysses. Edited with notes for schools. Boston, Ginn & Co., 1886. 16mo.

1890. Adventures of Ulysses. With an introduction by Andrew Lang. [Map.] London, [1890.] Square 12mo.

1830. Album Verses, with a few others, by Charles Lamb. [Engraved title.] London, 1830. 12mo.

1798. Blank Verse, by Charles Lamb and Charles Lloyd. London, 1798. 12mo.

[1811 ?] Beauty and the Beast; or, a Rough outside with a Gentle Heart. A poetical version of an ancient Tale. Illustrated with a series of

Elegant Engravings, and Beauty's Song at her Spinning-wheel, set to music by Mr. Whitaker. London, n.d. [1811?]. Square 24mo.

The First Edition.

1813. —— Another edition, 1813. 24mo.

1825. Beauty and the Beast; or, a Rough outside with a Gentle Heart, etc. London, William Jackson & Co., at the Juvenile Library, 195 St. Clemens, Strand, 1825. 3s. plain, 5s. colored.

1886. Beauty and the Beast; or, a Rough outside with a Gentle Heart. A Poem by Charles Lamb, now first reprinted from the original edition of 1811, with Preface and Notes by Richard Herne Shepherd. London, 1886. 12mo.

1887. Beauty and the Beast, by Charles Lamb, with an Introduction by Andrew Lang. Illustrated. London, n.d. [1887?]. Square 12mo. [Published with plates in two states.]

1823. Elia. Essays which have appeared under that signature in the London Magazine. London, 1823. 12mo.

The First Edition.

1828. Elia. Essays which have appeared under that signature in the London Magazine. Philadelphia, Carey, Lea, and Carey, 1828. 18mo.

The First American Edition. An exact reprint of the English.

1828. Elia. Essays which have appeared under that signature in the London Magazine. Second Series. Philadelphia, Carey, Lea, and Carey, 1828. 18mo.

A curious fact concerning this is that the second series was reprinted five years before the English Edition appeared. It was done by some one who did not know Lamb's style thoroughly, as several of his best Essays were not included, and others, not his, were, viz.: "Nuns and Ale of Caverswell," by Allan Cunningham, and "Valentine's Day," "Twelfth Night: or What you Will," by B. W. Procter.

1833. Elia. Essays which have appeared under that signature, etc. A New Edition. London, 1833. Post 8vo.

1835. Elia, etc. London, 1835. Post 8vo.

1838. Elia, etc. London, 1838. Post 8vo.

1840. Elia, etc. London, 1840. 12mo.

1833. [Elia.] Last Essays of Elia (The). Being a sequel to Essays pub-

lished under that name. [Second Series.] London, 1833. Small 8vo.
The First Edition, reprinted the same year in Philadelphia, 12mo.

1835. —— The Same. [Both Series.] A New Edition. London, 1835. 8vo. 2 vols.

1836. —— The Same. [Both Series.] A New Edition. London, 1836. 8vo.

1840. —— The Same. [Both Series.] Complete in One Volume. London, 1840. 12mo.
The series are paged separately.

1843. —— The Same. [Both Series.] A New Edition. Portrait. London, 1843. 8vo.
The edition was also issued in two volumes.

1845. Essays of Elia (The). [Library of Choice Reading.] New York, Wiley & Putnam, 1845. 2 vols. 12mo.

1847. —— The Same. [Both Series.] London, 1847. 12mo.

1849. —— The Same. [Both Series.] London, 1849. 12mo.

1852. —— The Same. [Both Series.] New York, 1852. 12mo.

1853. —— The Same. In Two Volumes. A New Edition. [Portrait.] London, 1853. 2 vols. 16mo.

1865. —— The Same. New Edition. New York, Widdleton, 1865. 8vo.

1867. —— The Same. A New Edition, with a Dedication and Preface hitherto unpublished, and a few Reminiscences by E. Oliver. London, J. C. Hotten, 1867. 8vo.

1867. —— The Same. London, Moxon, 1867. 12mo.

1867. Essays of Elia, and Eliana (The), with a Biographical Essay by H. S. London, 1867. 12mo.
Bohn's Standard Library.

1872. —— Another edition. London, 1872. 8vo.

1878. Essays of Elia. [Vest-Pocket Series.] Boston, 1878. 32mo.

1879. Essays of Elia, and Eliana, with a memoir by Barry Cornwall [B. W. Procter]. London, George Bell & Sons, 1879. 2 vols. 18mo.

1879. [Elia.] Twenty Selected Essays by G. H. Greene. London, 1879. 8vo.

1879. —— The Same. [Handy Volume Series.] N. Y., Appleton, 1879, 16mo.

1883. —— The Same, with Introduction and Notes by Alfred Ainger

London, Macmillan & Co., 1883. 12mo.

Reprinted 1884-1887, [with corrections and additions], 1888.

1883 Essays of Elia, by Charles Lamb. [Illustrated with etchings by R. Swain Gifford, James D. Smillie, Charles A Platt, F. S. Church.] [Islington Edition.] New York, 1883. 4to.

This edition was limited to 250 copies.

1884. —— The Same, reissued on thinner paper. 1884.

1885. —— Another edition. [Illustrated.] Edinburgh, 1885. 8vo.

1885. Essays of Elia and Other Pieces, with an Introduction by Henry Morley. [Morley's Universal Library.] London, 1885. 12mo.

The notes are by Charles Kent.

1886. [Elia.] Some Essays of Elia [with illustrations by C. O. Murray]. London, 1886. 8vo.

1886. Essays of Elia, etc., with a preface by H. R. Haweis. London, 1886. Square 16mo.

1887. —— The Same. London, 1887.
—— The Same. 1888.

1888. Essays of Elia (The), edited by Augustine Birrell [with etch-

ings by Herbert Railton. [The Temple Library]. London, J. M. Dent & Co., 1888. 2 vols. 24mo.

This edition was also made in Large Paper.

1889. Essays of Elia (The) [Illustrated from Photographs taken by Walter Collett.] London, David Stott, 1889. 32mo.

This was made also in Large Paper, only 100 copies printed.

1802. John Woodvil. A Tragedy; to which are added Fragments of Burton, the author of the Anatomy of Melancholy. London, 1802. 16mo.

The First Edition, incorporated in the Works thereafter.

1807. Mrs. Leicester's School; or, the History of Several Young Ladies related by themselves. London, 1807.

The First Edition.

1809. Mrs. Leicester's School; or, the History of Several Young Ladies related by themselves. The Second Edition. London, 1809. 16mo.

The Second Edition.

1810. Mrs. Leicester's School; or, the History of Several Young Ladies related by themselves. Third Edition. [Fron-

tispiece.] London, 1810. 16mo.
The Third Edition.

1814. —— The Same. London, 1814.
The Fourth Edition.

1825. Mrs. Leicester's School ; or, the History of Several Young Ladies related by themselves. Ninth Edition. [Frontispiece by Harvey.] London, 1825. 12mo.

1827. Mrs. Leicester's School ; or, the History of Several Young Ladies related by themselves. Tenth Edition. London, 1827.

1836. —— Another edition. London, 1836. Post 8vo.

1844. —— Another edition. London, 1844. 12mo.

1855. —— Another edition. London, 1855.

1881. —— Another edition, with illustrations. London, 1881. 8vo.

1884. Mrs. Leicester's School, etc. New Edition. London, 1884. 12mo.

1885. Mrs. Leicester's School and other writings in Prose and Verse, by Charles Lamb, with Introduction and Notes by Alfred Ainger. London, 1885. 12mo.

1809. Poetry for Children. Entirely original, by the author of " Mrs. Leicester's School." In two volumes. London, 1809. 2 vols. 12mo.
The First Edition.

1812. Poetry for Children. Entirely original, by the author of " Mrs. Leicester's School." Boston, West and Richardson, and Edward Cotton, 1812.
The first copy known, and the first American reprint.

1872. Poetry for Children, by Charles and Mary Lamb. Edited and prefaced by Richard Herne Shepherd. London, 1872. 16mo.

1877. Poetry for Children, by Charles and Mary Lamb. To which are added " Prince Dorus," and some uncollected Poems by Charles Lamb. Edited, Prefaced, and Annotated by Richard Herne Shepherd. London, Chatto & Windus, 1877. 12mo.

1877. —— The Same. Reprinted. New York, 1877. Charles Scribner's Sons. 16mo.

1889. Poetry for Children, by Charles and Mary Lamb. To which are added " Prince Dorus," and some uncollected Poems by Charles Lamb. Edited, Prefaced, and Annotated by Rich ard Herne Shepherd. New York, 1889. 16mo.

An exact reprint of the edition of 1877.

1811. [?] Prince Dorus; or. Flattery put out of Countenance. A Poetical version of an Ancient Tale. Illustrated with a series of Elegant Engravings. London, 1811. 12mo.

The First Edition.

1877. [Prince Dorus.] Poetry for Children, by Charles and Mary Lamb. To which are added "Prince Dorus." and some uncollected Poems by Charles Lamb. Edited, Prefaced, and Annotated by Richard Herne Shepherd. London, Chatto & Windus, 1877. 12mo.

1889. Prince Dorus, by Charles Lamb. With Nine Illustrations in facsimile (hand-coloured). London, Field & Tuer, 1889. 8vo.

Only 500 copies printed, each numbered. This contains an Introduction by A. W. T. [A. W. Tuer], and is an exact fac-simile of the original edition.

1835. Recollections of Christ's Hospital, by the late Charles Lamb. originally published in 1813, now reprinted by some of his school-fellows and friends, etc. London, 1835. 8vo.

1831. Satan in Search of a Wife; with the whole process of his Courtship and Marriage, and who danced at the wedding, by an Eye-Witness. London, 1831. 12mo.

The First Edition.

1808. Specimens of English Dramatic Poets, who lived about the time of Shakespeare, with Notes, by Charles Lamb. London, 1808. 12mo.

The First Edition.

1813. Specimens of English Dramatic Poets, who lived about the time of Shakespeare, with Notes. Second Edition. London, John Bumpus, 1813.

The Second Edition.

1814. Specimens of English Dramatic Poets, who lived about the time of Shakespeare, with Notes. London, 1814. Moxon. 2 vols. 12mo.

1835. Specimens of English Dramatic Poets, who lived about the time of Shakespeare, with Notes. A new edition. In two volumes. London, 1835. 16mo.

1844. Specimens of English Dramatic Poets, of about the time of

Shakespeare, etc.
London, 1844. 2 vols.

1845. —— Another edition.
New York, 1845. 2
vols. in 1.

1847. Specimens of English
Dramatic Poets, who
lived about the time
of Shakespeare, with
Notes, by C h a r l e s
Lamb. A new edition,
including the extracts
from the G a r r i c k
Plays. [Bohn's Anti-
quarian L i b r a r y.]
London, 1847. 12mo.

This edition contains a
short Prefatory note by
H. G. Bohn.

1852. ——The same. London,
1852. Crown 8vo.

1854. Specimens of English
Dramatic Poets, etc.
London, 1854. Crown
8vo.

1854. Specimens of English
Dramatic Poets, etc.
N. Y., W. P. Hazard,
1854. 12mo.

1798. Tale of Rosamund Gray
and Old Blind Mar-
g a r e t (A). London,
1798. 12mo.

1835. Tale of Rosamund Gray,
R e c o l l e c t i o n s of
Christ's Hospital (A),
etc., etc. London,
1835. 8vo.

1838. Tale of Rosamund Gray
and Old Blind Mar-
garet (A). etc. Lon-
don, 1838. 8vo.

1841. Tale of Rosamund Gray
and Old Blind Mar-

garet (A). London
1841. 12mo.

Essays, Letters, etc.
[Double column.]

1849. Tale of Rosamund Gray,
etc. London, 1849.
12mo.

1850. Tale of Rosamund Gray,
etc. (Bohn.) London,
1850. 12mo.

1807. Tales from Shakespear,
designed for the Use
of Young Persons, by
Charles Lamb. Em-
bellished with Copper-
Plates. In two vol-
umes. London, 1807.
2 vols. 12mo.

The First Edition.

1809. Tales from Shakespear,
designed for the Use
of Young Persons.
[20 plates, engraved
by Blake.] [Portrait
of Shakespeare.] Lon-
don, 1809. 2 vols.
12mo.

The Second Edition.

1810. —— Another edition.
London. 12mo. 2
vols.

1813. Tales from Shakespear,
designed for the Use
of Young Persons.
Philadelphia, Brad-
f o r d and Inskeep,
1813. 2 vols. 12mo.

The First American
Edition.

1816. Tales from Shakespear,
designed for the Use
of Young Persons.
The Third Edition.
[20 plates, engraved

by Blake]. London 1816. 2 vols. 12mo.
This edition contains the "Advertisement" to the second, but is in other respects a reprint.

1822. Tales from Shakespear, designed for the Use of Young Persons. The Fourth Edition. London, 1822. 2 vols. 12mo.
The Fourth Edition, omitting the "Advertisement."

1831. Tales from Shakespeare, designed for the Use of Young Persons [with designs by Harvey]. London, Moxon, 1831. 12mo.
The Fifth Edition, the printers being changed from M. J. Godwin to Moxon.

1837. —— Another edition. London, 1837. 12mo.

1838. Tales from Shakespeare, designed for the Use of Young Persons, by Mr. and Miss Lamb. Sixth Edition, ornamented with designs by Harvey. London, Baldwin and Cradock, 1838.
The Sixth Edition.

1839. Tales from Shakespeare. London, Baldwin [Godwin], 1839. 12mo.

1843. Tales from Shakespeare. London, H. G. Bohn, 1843. 12mo.

1844. Tales from Shakespeare. London, 1844, Groombridge. 32mo.
—— The Same. Lon-

don, 1844, Cox. 2 vols. 18mo.
—— The Same. London, Moxon, 1844. 24mo.

1846. Tales from Shakespeare, with vocabulary. compiled by E. Amthor. Leipsic, 1846. 16mo.

1859. Tales from Shakespeare. Edited by Charles Knight. London, 1859, Griffin. 18mo.
Reprinted, London, 1865. 12mo.

1861. Tales from Shakespeare. London, 1861, Bell & Daldy. 24mo.

1863. Tales from Shakespeare, with woodcuts, by Harvey. London, 1863. 12mo.

1864. Tales from Shakespeare. New York, F. H. Dodd, 1864. 32mo.

1864. Tales from Shakespeare. New York, Hurd & Houghton, 1864. 12mo.

1865. Tales from Shakespeare. London, 1865. 12mo.

1866. —— Another edition. London, 1866. 8vo.

1867. Tales from Shakespeare. London, Routledge, 1867.

1873. —— Another edition. London, 1873. 8vo.

1875. Tales from Shakespeare. [Illustrated.] London, 1875. 12mo.

1876. Tales from Shakespeare. London, Barrett, 1876. Crown 8vo.

1877. Tales from Shakespeare. [Half - Hour Series.] N. Y., Harper Bros., 1877. 32mo.

1877. Tales from Shakespeare. London, Lockwood, 1877. 12mo.

1877. Tales from Shakespeare. [Little Classics.] Boston, Osgood. 18mo.

1877. Tales from Shakespeare. New edition. [Illustrated by Gilbert.] London, 1877. 16mo.

1878. Tales from Shakespeare. [Illustrated.] London, 1878, Chatto & Windus. 4to.

1878. Tales from Shakespeare. London, Warne, 1878.

1878. Tales from Shakespeare. With twelve illustrations in permanent photography from the Boydell Gallery. London, Bickers & Son, 1878. Crown 8vo.

1879. Tales from Shakespeare. London, 1879. 2 vols. 12mo.

1879. Tales from Shakespeare. London, Whittaker. 1879. 32mo.

1879. Tales from Shakespeare, by Charles and Mary Lamb. Edited, with an Introduction, by Alfred Ainger. London, Macmillan & Co. [Golden Treasury Series.] 16mo.
 Reprinted, 1883, 1886, in 12mo.

—— Another edition. London, 1887.

1879. —— Another edition. London, 1879. 4to.

1881. Tales from Shakespeare. [Colored Plates.] London, Routledge, 1881. 12mo.

1881. Tales from Shakespeare. [Illustrated Chandos Classics.] London, Warne, 1881. 12mo.

1882. Tales from Shakespeare. [Illustrated by Gilbert.] London, 1882, Routledge. 4to.

1883. Tales from Shakespeare. Edited by Ainger. London, 1883. 12mo.

1883. —— Another edition. Edited by Alfred Ainger. [Globe Readings.] London, 1883. 12mo.

1885. Tales from Shakespeare, designed for the Use of Young Persons. 16th Edition. [With steel Portrait. Engravings by Harvey.] London, 1885. Lockwood. 12mo.

1886. —— Another edition. [Routledge's World Library.] 1886. 16mo.

1888. Tales from Shakespeare, by Charles and Mary Lamb. [Chiswick Series.] London, 1888. 18mo.

1888. —— Another edition. Edited by A. Gardiner. [Heywood's Literary Readers.] London, 1888. 8vo.

VII. LETTERS.

1837. The Letters of Charles Lamb, with a Sketch of his Life, by Thomas Noon Talfourd, one of his executors. In two volumes. [Portraits.] London, Edward Moxon, 1837. 2 vols. 8vo.

> The Letters in this edition are not published entire. A mistaken scrupulousness prompted the omission of much.

1848. The Final Memorials of Charles Lamb : consisting chiefly of his Letters not before published, with Sketches by some of his contemporaries, by Thomas Noon Talfourd, one of his executors. In two volumes. London, Edward Moxon, 1848.

> Not published until after Mary's death. The first full-length portrait of Lamb the public had obtained.

1849. —— Another edition. London, Moxon, 1849. 12mo.
—— Another Edition. Appleton, New York. 1849. 12mo.

1850. —— Another edition. London, 1850. 12mo.

1854. ——The Same. Life and Letters, etc., etc. Phila-

delphia. W. P. Hazard, 1854. 12mo.

1886. Letters of Charles Lamb, with some account of the writer, his friends and correspondents, and explanatory notes, by the late Sir Thomas Noon Talfourd, one of his executors. An entirely new edition. Carefully revised and greatly enlarged by W. Carew Hazlitt. London, George Bell & Sons, 1886. 2 vols. 12mo.

> Printed in Bohn Library. This edition contains Talfourd's original prefaces, and gives the Letters in full but rearranged, with additions, freely interspersed with original matter. They are also arranged chronologically.

1888. The Letters of Charles Lamb, newly arranged, with additions, edited, with Introductions and Notes, by Alfred Ainger. [Portrait.] London, Macmillan & Co., 1888. 2 vols. 12mo.

> The recension of the Manning and Barton correspondence, a set of letters to Dibdin, a letter to Chambers and Dodwell, and a complete chronological arrangement of the Letters are the chief features of this, by all means, best edition.

VIII. POETICAL WORKS.

1836. The Poetical Works of Charles Lamb. A new edition. London, Edward Moxon, 1836. 8vo.

The first edition in separate form. Those in italics are by Mary. Contents : Poems, Sonnets, Blank Verse, Album Verses.

1838. The Poetical Works of Charles Lamb. Third Edition. London, Moxon, 1838. 16mo.

An exact reprint of the edition of 1836.

1839. —— The Same. London, 1839. Medium 8vo.

1840. —— The Same. London, 1840. 12mo.

1842. —— The Same. London, Bohn. 1842. 12mo.

1849. —— The Same. London, 1848. 8vo.

1852. —— The Same. Philadelphia, 1852. 8vo.

1884. Poems, Plays, and Miscellaneous Essays, with Notes and Introduction by Alfred Ainger. London, Macmillan & Co., 1884. 12mo.

IX. LAMBIANA.

BIOGRAPHY, CRITICISMS, ETC.

Ainger (Alfred). Charles Lamb [English Men of Letters Series]. London, 1882. 16mo.

Ainger (Alfred). Charles Lamb. London, 1888. 12mo.

Rewritten and enlarged from the former work.

Allibone (S. A.). Critical Dictionary of English Literature and British and American authors. Philadelphia, 1870. 3 vols. 8vo.

Vol. II. Article : Charles Lamb.

Allsop (Thomas). Letters, Conversations, and Recollections of S. T.

Coleridge. London, 1836. 2 vols. 12mo.

This contains many items of interest concerning Lamb.

American Cyclopedia (Appleton's). New York, 1873. 16 vols. 8vo.

Article : Charles Lamb.

Babson (J. E.). Eliana : being the hitherto uncollected writings of Charles Lamb. New York and Boston, 1865. 12mo.

Contents : Preface. Essays and Sketches, The Pawnbroker's Daughter. The Adventures of Ulysses. Tales, Poems.

Balmanno (Mary). Pen and Pencil. New York, 1858. Square 8vo. Pp. 121-146.

Barton (Bernard). Memoirs, Letters, and Poems of. Edited by his daughter. Philadelphia, 1856. 12mo. Charles Lamb, pp. 168-184.

Bates (William). The Maclise Portrait Gallery of "Illustrious Literary Characters," with Memoirs, etc. London, 1883. 8vo. Charles Lamb, pp. 290-300.

[Birrell (Augustine).] Obiter Dicta. [Second Series] London, 1887. 12mo. Charles Lamb, pp. 222-256. A review of "Works" reprinted from *Macmillan's Magazine.*

Blessington (Countess of). The Literary Life and Correspondence of. Edited by R. R. Madden. London, 1855. 3 vols. 8vo. Vol. II. p. 369; Vol. III. p. 176.

Bric à Brac Series [edited by R. H. Stoddard]. Personal Recollections of Lamb, Hazlitt, and others. New York, 1875. 12mo. Introductory Preface, p. 1-47.

Letters, etc. This was a valuable addition to the knowledge of Lamb.

Bulwer-Lytton (E. L.). Prose Works. London, 1868. 3 vols. 12mo. Vol. I. pp. 89-123.

Calvert (George H.). The Gentleman. Boston, 1861. 12mo. Pp. 32-42.

Carlyle (Thomas). A History of the First Forty Years of his Life, 1795-1835. By J. A. Froude. London, 1882. 2 vols. 8vo. Vol. I. p. 222; Vol. II. pp. 203, 210.

Chambers's Cyclopedia of English Literature. London, 1876. 2 vols. 8vo. Vol. II. pp. 90-95.

Chambers's Encyclopedia, etc. Revised Edition. Edinburgh, 1882. 8vo. Article: Charles Lamb.

Chorley (H. F.) The Authors of England. A series of Medallion Portraits, etc. London, 1838. 4to. Charles Lamb.

Clarke (Charles and Mary Cowden). Recollections of Writers, with Letters. New York, 1878. 12mo. Charles Lamb and his Letters Mary Lamb. pp. 158-189.

Clarke (F. L.). Golden Friendships, etc. London, 1884. 8vo. Lamb and Coleridge, pp. 160-185.

Clayden (P. W.). Rogers and his Contemporaries. London, 1886. 2 vols. Crown 8vo.
Vol. I. p. 350.

Coleridge (S. T.). Life of, by Hall Caine [Great Writers' Series.] London, 1887. 8vo.
Numerous references to Charles Lamb.

Collins (Stephen). Autobiography and Miscellanies. Philadelphia, 1872. 12mo.
P. 39.

Cottle (Joseph). Reminiscences of Samuel Taylor Coleridge and Robert Southey. London, 1847. 12mo.
Frequent mention of Lamb.

Craddock (Thomas). Charles Lamb. Liverpool. 1867. 12mo.

Craik (G. L.). Compendious History of English Literature, &c. New York, 1875. 12mo.
Vol. II. pp. 478, 534, 553, 554, 555.

Cunningham (Allan). Biographical and Critical History of the Literature of the last Fifty Years. [Waldie's Library, Vol. III.] Philadelphia, 1833-1849. 12 vols. 16mo.

Daniel (George). Love's Last Labor not Lost. London, 1863. 16mo.
Recollections of Charles Lamb, pp. 1-31.

De Quincey (Thomas). Biographical Essays. 1851. 12mo.
Pp 167-228.

—— Literary Reminiscences. Boston, 1852. 2 vols. 12mo.
Vol. I. pp. 62-135.

Elliston (R. W.). The Life and Enterprise of. By George Raymond. London, 1857. 12mo.
Pp. 266, etc.

Encyclopedia Britannica. The Encyclopedia Britannica. Eighth Edition. Edinburgh, 1856. 4to.
Article: Lamb, by R. Carruthers.

—— The Same. Ninth Edition. Edinburgh. 1876. 4to.
Article: Charles Lamb.

English Cyclopedia. A new Dictionary of Universal Knowledge. (Charles Knight's.)
Article: Charles Lamb.

English Poets (The). Selections, with Critical Introductions, etc. [Edited by T. H. Ward.] London, 1889. 4 vols. 12mo.
Charles Lamb, Vol. IV. pp. 326-333.

Fields (James T.). Yesterdays with Authors. Boston, 1871. 12mo.
The Article: "Barry Cornwall and some of his Friends," contains numerous references to Lamb and his sister.

Fitzgerald (Percy). Afternoon Lectures. Second Series. London, 1864. 12mo.
Vol. II. pp. 67-101.

—— Art of the Stage (The), as set out in Lamb's Dramatic Essays, with a Commentary. London, 1885. 12mo.

—— Charles Lamb: His Friends, his Haunts, and his Books. [Portraits.] London, 1866. Square 12mo.

—— Little Essays, Sketches, and Characters, by C. L. Selected from his Letters. London, 1884. 12mo.

—— Recreations of a London Literary Man. London, 1882. 2 vols. 12mo.
Vol. I. p. 235.

Fox (Caroline). Memoirs of Old Friends, etc., 1835-1871. Edited by H. N. Pym. London, 1882. 8vo.
Mentions Lamb, pp. 12, 19, 46, 52, 145.

Francis (John). Literary Chronicle of a Half Century. London, 1882. 2 vols. 12mo.
Frequent mention of Lamb and his connection with *The Athenæum*.

Gilchrist (Mrs.). Mary Lamb. [Famous Women Series.] 16mo. London, W. H. Allen, 1883. 16mo.
Numerous mention of her brother.

Gilfillan (George). A Gallery of Literary Portraits. London, 1845-54. 3 vols. 12mo.
Vol. I. pp. 338-345. Sketch of Lamb, with Portrait.

Godwin (William). His Friends and Acquaintances. By C. Kegan Paul. London, 1876. 2 vols. 8vo.
Vol. I., p. 362; Vol. II., p. 321.

Hall (S. C.). Retrospect of a Long Life. From 1815 to 1883. London, 1883. 2 vols. 8vo.
Vol. II. contains Anecdotes, etc., of Lamb.

Hall (Mr. and Mrs. S. C.). Memories of Great Men and Women. London, 1876. 8vo.
P. 11.

Haydon (B. R.). Life of. Edited by Tom Taylor. London, 1853. 3 vols. 12mo.
Numerous references to Lamb.

Hazlitt (W. Carew). Mary and Charles Lamb. Poems, Letters, and Remains. Now first collected. With Reminiscences and Notes. Portraits, Fac-similes, and Illustrations. London, 1874. 4to.
Unusually interesting and important, containing matter not in

any of the earlier edi-
tions. Issued also in
8vo.

—— Spirit of the Age ; or,
Contemporary Por-
traits. London, 1825.
12mo.

Pp. 395-405.

—— Table Talk. London,
1845-6. 2 vols.
16mo.

Vol. II. On Conversation
of Authors.

—— Memoirs. With Por-
tions of his Corre-
spondence. By W. C.
Hazlitt. London,
1867. 2 vols. 12mo.
References to Lamb.

—— Literary Remains. By
his Son. London,
1836. 2 vols. 12mo.
References to C. L.

Hood (Thomas). Memorials, by
his Daughter. Lon-
don, 1860. 2 vols.
12mo.

Howitt (William). The Northern Heights of Lon-
don. London, 1869.
8vo.

Pp. 882-885.

Hunt (Leigh). Lord Byron
and Some of his
Contemporaries, etc.
London, 1828. 4to.

Charles Lamb, pp. 296,
299. [With Portrait by
Meyer.]

—— Autobiography. With
Reminiscences of
Friends and Contem-
poraries. London,
1850. 3 vols. 12mo.

Numerous references to
Lamb.

Hutton (Laurence). Literary
Landmarks of Lon-
don. Boston, 1885.
12mo.

Pp. 182-193. The most
accurate account ex-
tant.

Imperial Dictionary of Universal Biography (The).
Glasgow, n.d. 8vo.

Vol. III. Article:
Charles Lamb, by
Charles Taylor.

Imitation of Celebrated Au-
thors ; or, Imaginary
Rejected Articles.
London, 1844. 12mo.

P. 30 contains imitation
of Lamb.

Ireland (Alexander). List of
the writings of Wil-
liam Hazlitt and
Leigh Hunt, etc., pre-
ceded by a review of,
and extracts from Bar-
ry Cornwall's "Me-
morials of Charles
Lamb," etc., and a
chronological list of
the works of Charles
Lamb. London :
1868. 12mo.

Pp. 3-26. Charles Lamb.

Jesse (J. Heneage). London,
its celebrities, charac-
ters, and remarkable
places. London, 1851.
3 vols. 12mo.

Vol. I. pp. 330, 345, 388;
Vol. III. pp. 220, 228,
313.

Johnson's Universal Cyclopædia, etc. New
York, 1886. 2 vols.
8vo.

Article, Charles Lamb.
P. C. Bliss.

Mathews (William). The Great Conversers and other Essays. Chicago, 1876. 12mo.

Pp. 32, 117, 165, 173.

Macmillan (Daniel). Memoirs of. By Thomas Hughes. London, 1822. 12mo.

P. 141.

Mathews (Charles). Life and Correspondence, etc. Edited by his Widow. London, 1838. 4 vols. 8vo.

Numerous references to Lamb.

Minto (William), A Manual of English Prose Literature, etc. London, 1886. 12mo.

Pp. 537, 539.

Moir (D. M.), Sketches of the Poetical Literature of the past Half Century. Edinburgh, 1851. 16mo.

Moore (Thomas). Journal and Correspondence. Edited by Lord John Russell. London, 1853. 8 vols. 8vo.

Lamb Anecdotes, etc., Vol. III. p. 136; Vol. IV. pp. 50, 51 : Vol. V. p. 317; Vol. VI. p. 249.

Munden (J. S.). Memoirs of. By his Son. London, 1844. 8vo.

Refers to Charles Lamb.

Mylius (W. F.). The First Book of Poetry for the Use of Schools,

etc. London, 1815. 16mo.

This contains selections from " Poetry for Children."

Notes and Queries. General Index to Notes and Queries. Seven Series. London, 1856, 1890 4to.

Numerous references to Lamb.

Oliphant (Mrs.). Literary History of England. London, 1889. 3 vols. 8vo.

Vol. I. pp. 230, 250; Vol. II. pp. 65, 176, 177, 250, etc. ; Vol. III. 1, 7, 240.

Pater (W. H.). Appreciations, with an Essay on Style. London, 1889. 12mo.

Pp. 107-126, Charles Lamb.

Patmore (P. G.). My Friends and Acquaintances. London, 1884. 4 vols. 12mo.

Numerous and most important references to, and reminiscences of Lamb.

[Patmore (P. G.).] Rejected Articles. London, 1826. 12mo.

Contains imitation of Lamb.

Pen and Ink Sketches of Poets, Preachers, and Politicians. [By John Dix.] London, 1846. 8vo.

Lamb and Coleridge, pp. 122, 140.

Penny Cyclopædia (The)

188

Bibliography.

[Chas. Knight's.] London, 1839. 8vo. Vol. XIII. Article: Charles Lamb.

Personal Traits of British Authors — Wordsworth, Coleridge, Lamb, Hazlitt, Leigh Hunt, Procter. Edited by E. T. Mason. New York, 1885. 12mo.
Pp. 113-173. Charles Lamb.

Poole (Thomas). Thomas Poole and his Friend. By Mrs. Sandford. London, 1888. 12mo. 2 vols. 8vo.
Numerous references to Charles Lamb.

Procter (B.W.). Charles Lamb. A Memoir, by Barry Cornwall. London, 1868. 8vo.
This contains portraits theretofore unknown.

Robinson (Henry Crabb). Diary, Reminiscences, and Correspondence, selected and edited by Thomas Sadler. London, 1866. 3 vols. 8vo.
This is crowded with references to Lamb and his sister.

Russell (W. Clark). The Book of Authors. London, 1876. 8vo.
Pp. 71, 105, 144, 204, 392, 399, 427, 447.

St. Albans (Duchess of). Memoirs of Miss Mellon, by Mrs. C. Barron-

Wilson. London, 1840. 2 vols. 12mo.
Account of the production of "Mr. H."—a Farce. Vol I. p. 296.

Shaw (Thomas B.). Complete Manual of English Literature, etc. New York, 1867. 12mo.
Pp. 470-472.

Southey (Robert). Life and Correspondence. Edited by C. C. Southey. London, 1850. 6 vols. 8vo.
Many references to Lamb.

Swinburne (A. C.). "William Blake," a critical Essay. London, 1868. 8vo.
P. 8.

—— Miscellanies. London, 1886. 12mo.
Charles Lamb and George Wither, pp. 152-200. Originally published in the Nineteenth Century.

Taine, H. A. History of English Literature. Translated by H. Van Laun. London, 1886. 4 vols. 8vo.
Charles Lamb, Vol. III. pp. 423-427.

Thompson (Mrs. K. B.). Celebrated Friendships. London, 1881. 2 vols. 12mo.
Vol. II. pp. 53-98.

Ticknor (George). Life, Letters, and Journals of. [Edited by G. S. Hilliard, George Stillman, and others.]

Boston, 1876. 2 vols. 8vo.

Vol. I. p. 294, contains a curious account of an evening with Lamb.

Timbs (J.). Anecdote Lives of the Later Wits and Humourists. London, 1874. 2 vols. 12mo.

Vol. I. contains numerous allusions, etc., to Lamb.

Trollope (Wm.). A History of the Royal Foundation of Christ's Hospital, with an account of the plan of education, etc., and Memoirs of Eminent Blues, etc. London, 1834. 4to.

Numerous references to Lamb.

Tuckerman (H. T.). Characteristics of Literature. First Series. Philadelphia, 1849. 12mo.

Pp. 130, 170. Charles Lamb, the Humourist.

Universal Pronouncing Diction-ary of Biography and Mythology. [Edited by Joseph Thomas.] Philadelphia, 1889. 4to.

Article: Charles Lamb

Wainewright (Thomas Griffiths). Essays and Criticisms. Now first collected, with some account of the author, by W. C. Hazlitt. London, 1880. 12mo.

Numerous references to Lamb.

Wilson (John). Noctes Ambrosianæ. New York, 1863. 5 vols. 8vo.

Vol. I. pp. 170, 224; Vol. II. p. 106.

Willis (N. P.). Pencillings by the Way. New York. 1853. 12mo.

Wordsworth (William). Life, by William Knight. Edinburgh, 1889. 3 vols. 8vo.

Full of references to Charles Lamb.

MAGAZINE ARTICLES.

Lamb (Charles). *Overland Monthly* (N. S.), Vol. IV. p. 284, H. Colbach. — *The Academy*, Vol. XXI. p. 168, R. C. Browne. — *The Athenæum*, Vol. II. p. 566 (1886), A. Ainger. — *Eclectic Magazine*, Vol. XXIII. p. 491; Vol. XXXI. p. 390. — *Fraser's Magazine*, Vol. LXXV. p. 657, G. Massey. — *Living Age* (Littell's), Vol. L. p. 145; Vol. LXI. p. 771. — *Monthly Review*, Vol. XC. p. 253; Vol. CXXXVIII. p. 110; Vol. CXLIII. p. 467. — *Modern Review*, Vol. C. pp. 1-202. — *Methodist Quarterly Review*, Vol. XVIII. p. 566, W. H. Barnes. — *Macmillan's*

Magazine, Vol. XXIX. p. 431, A. Black.—*New England Magazine*, Vol. IX. p. 233.—*People's Journal*, Vol. XI. p. 357.—*Pioneer (The)*, Vol. II. p. 144, C. H. Washburn. — *Southern Literary Messenger*, Vol. VI. p. 652. —*Sharpe's London Magazine*, Vol. XXVIII. p. 239. —*All the Year Round*, Vol. XXXV. p. 275. — *Canada Monthly*, Vol. XVII. p. 350, -J. C. Duncan.—*Dial (The)* [Chicago], Vol. IX. p. 38. E. G. Johnson.—*Every Saturday*, Vol. XII. p. 292.— *Gentleman's Magazine* (N. S.), Vol. XLI. p. 55, W. Summers.—*Hogg's Weekly Instructor*, Vol. XI. p. 145. *Tait's Edinburgh Magazine* (N. S.), Vol. IV. p. 575; Vol. V. pp. 237-559, De Quincey ; Vol. XV. p. 782.— *Universalist Quarterly*, Vol. II. p. 289, M. Davis ; Vol. XI. p. 90, J. Washburne ; Vol. XVII. p. 113, A. L. Barry.—*Harper's Magazine*, Vol. XXI. p. 811 ; Vol. LIV. p. 916 ; Vol. LV. p. 464 [Easy Chair].

—— A Memoir. By Barry Cornwall. *British Quarterly Review*, Vol. XLV. p. 335.—*Living Age* [Littell's], Vol. XC. p. 771. — *Edinburgh Review*, Vol. CXXIV. p. 261.

—— About Essayists and Reviewers.—Charles Lamb. *Bentley's Magazine*, Vol. XXIX. p. 430.

—— About. *Eclectic Magazine*, Vol. LXXVIII. p. 675. — *Temple Bar*, Vol. LXXXV. p. 33.

—— An Autobiographical Sketch. *New Monthly Magazine* [Colburn's], Vol. XLIII. p. 499.

—— Ainger's Life of. *The Academy*, Vol. XXI. p. 168, R. C. Browne.—*The Athenæum*, Vol. I. p. 371 [1882].

—— and Dr. Johnson. *Temple Bar*, Vol. LXXXVI. p. 237, P. W. Roose.

—— and George Wither. *Nineteenth Century*, Vol. XVII. p. 66, A. C. Swinburne.

—— and Hood. *Christian Examiner*, Vol. LXIX. p. 415, T. B. Fox.

—— and his Friends. *Fraser's Magazine*, Vol. CV. p. 606, J. Dennis. — *North American Review*, Vol. CIV. p. 3863.

—— and his Sister. *Eclectic Magazine*, Vol. XV. p. 257.

—— and Joseph Cottle. *The Athenæum*, Vol. II. p. 468 [1886], A. Ainger. — The Same, Vol. II. p. 535 [1886], R. H. Shepherd. — The Same, Vol. II. p. 566 [1886], A. Ainger.

—— and Keats. *Southern Literary Messenger*, Vol. XIV. p. 711, H. T. Tuckerman.

—— and Mary. *Tinsley's Magazine*, Vol. XXXVIII. p. 496.—*The Dial* [Chicago], Vol. IV. p. 110, F. F. Browne.

—— and Mary Lamb, their

Editors and Biographers. *Westminster Review*, Vol. CII. p. 419.
—— and Sydney Smith. *Atlantic Monthly*, Vol. III. p. 290, W. L. Symonds.
—— and Thomas Carlyle. *New England Magazine*, Vol. XLIV. p. 605, N. W. Wells.
—— Another Dish of Lamb. *Old and New Magazine*, Vol. X. p. 613, J. E. Babson.
—— at Edmonton. *Dublin University Magazine* (N. S.), Vol. VII. p. 469. — The Same, Vol. XCII. p. 467, H. F. Cox.
—— at his Desk. *Gentleman's Magazine* (N. S.), Vol. VI. p. 285. C. Pebody.
—— Books of. *Historical Magazine*, Vol. IX. p. 45.
—— Boyhood of. *Dublin University Magazine*, Vol. LXXIX. p. 149.
—— Character of the Humourist—Charles Lamb. *Fortnightly*, Vol. XXX. p. 466, W. H. Pater.
—— Concerning. *Scribner's Monthly*, Vol. II. p. 720, J. H. Twitchell.
—— Discovery of Lamb's 'Poetry for Children." *Gentleman's Magazine* (N. S.), Vol. XIX. p. 113, R. H. Shepherd.
—— Dramatic Attempts of. *Lippincott's Magazine*, Vol. XXI. p. 493, J. Brander Matthews.
—— Essays of Elia. *American Quarterly Review*, Vol. XIX. p. 185, H. T. Tuckerman.—*Museum of Foreign Literature* [Littell's], Vol. IV. p. 33.—*Quarterly Review*, Vol. LIV. p. 58, "E. B." [Bulwer.]—*Methodist Review*, Vol. XLVII. p. 382, D. Wise.
—— Eliana [with a Portrait]. *London Society*, Vol. XLII. p. 182.
—— Fairy Tales in Verse, by. *Gentleman's Magazine* (N. S.), Vol. XXXV. p. 188.
—— Final Memorials [edited by Talfourd]. *British Quarterly Review*, Vol. VIII. p. 381.—*Christian Remembrancer*, Vol. XVI. p. 424.—*New Monthly Magazine* (Colburn's), Vol. LXXXIII. p. 532.—*North British Review*, Vol. X. p. 179.
—— Genius and Character of. *Westminster Review*, Vol. CXXVI. p. 16.
—— Gleanings from his Biographers. *Macmillan's Magazine*, Vol. XV. p. 473.
—— Grave of. *Living Age* [Littell's], Vol. LXXIV. p. 316.
—— His Friends, his Haunts, and his Books. *British Quarterly Review*, Vol. XLV. p. 335.
—— His Last Words on Coleridge. *New Monthly Magazine* (Colburn's).
—— Humour of. *Gentleman's Magazine* (N. S.), Vol. XXVI. p. 699, A. H. Japp.
—— In the Footprints of. *Scribner's Magazine*, Vol. VII. pp. 267, 471. E. E. Martin.

—— John Woodvil. *Edinburgh Review.* Vol. II. p. 90.

—— Last Records of. *Chambers's Journal*, Vol. XLIII. p. 763.

—— Leigh Hunt and. *The Athenæum*, Vol. I. p. 344 [1889], A. Ainger.—The Same. Vol. I. p. 374 [1889], E. Gosse.—The Same, Vol. I. p. 108, Ainger.—J. A. C. Cox. II. R. Fox-Bourne.

—— Letters [edited by Ainger]. *The Academy*, Vol. XXXIII. p. 265, R. C. Browne.—*The Athenæum*, Vol. I. p. 427 [1887], The *Spectator*, Vol. LXI. p. 754. —*Saturday Review*, Vol. LXV. p. 453.—*Macmillan's Magazine*, Vol. LV. p. 161, A. Ainger.—The Same, Vol. LVIII. p. 95, A. Birrell.

—— Letters [edited by Hazlitt]. *The Athenæum*, Vol. I. p. 474 [1884].—*The Spectator*, Vol. LIX. p. 1242.

—— Letters [edited by Talfourd]. *British and Foreign Review*, Vol. V. p. 507. —*American Quarterly Review*, Vol. XXII. p. 473.— *American Whig Review*, Vol. LIII. p. 381, G. W. Peck.—*Eclectic Review*, Vol. LXVI. p. 380.—*Edinburgh Review*, Vol. LXVI. p. 1.— *North American Review*, Vol. XLVI. p. 55, C. C. Felton.—*New York Review*, Vol. II. p. 213.—*Westminster Review*, Vol. XXVII. p. 229. — *American Monthly Magazine*, Vol. II. p. 73.

—— Letter of Elia to Robert

Southey, *Museum of Foreign Literature*, Vol. II. p. 561.

—— Lord Byron, words with. *Harper's Magazine*, Vol. I. p. 272 [1850].

—— Matilda Betham, Letters of Coleridge, Southey, and Lamb to. *Fraser's Magazine*, Vol. XCVIII. p. 73, "B.E." [Betham-Edwards?]

—— New English Edition of Works. *Atlantic Monthly*, Vol. XXVII. p. 745.

—— Notes of, to Thomas Allsop. *Harper's Magazine* [December, 1859. Edited by G. W. Curtis.]

—— On the Economy of. *Knickerbocker Magazine*, Vol. XXXIX. p. 347, F. W. Shelton.

—— Recollections of. *The Athenæum*, January 24, February 7, 1833.—*Living Age* [Littell's], Vol. LX. p. 381.

—— Reviewing Oneself. *The Athenæum*, Vol. II. p. 164 [1886], J. D. Campbell.

—— Robert Southey. *Bentley's Magazine*, Vol. XXXVI. p. 603.

—— Some Letters of, with Reminiscences of Himself awakened by. *Gentleman's Magazine* (N. S.), Vol. XI. p. 617, M. C. Clarke.

—— Tales from Shakespeare. *The Portfolio* (Dennie's), Vol. X. p. 472 [1813].—*The Spectator*, Vol. LVIII. p. 162.

—— Tribute to his Memory. *The Athenæum*, January 3, 1835, B. W. Procter.

—— Two neglected Letters of. *The Critic*, Vol. XIII. p. 167.

—— Uncollected Writings. *Atlantic Monthly*, Vol. XI. p. 529 —The Same, Vol. XII. p. 401.—The Same, Vol. XIV. pp. 478-552, J. E. Babson.

—— Works. *American Whig Review*, Vol. VII. p. 508, J. H. Barrett. — *Blackwood's Magazine*, Vol. III. p. 599.— The Same, Vol. LVI. p. 133. —*British Quarterly Review*, Vol. VII. p. 292 ; Vol. XLV. p. 335.—*Boston Quarterly*, Vol. IV. p. 214. [" B.A.B "]. —*Christian Examiner*, Vol. XXXIII. p. 434. W. H. Furness.—*Living Age* [Littell's], Vol. LX. p. 771.— *Macmillan's Magazine*, Vol. LIV. p. 276, A. Birrell.

—— Writings of. *Knickerbocker Magazine*, Vol. XXXV. p. 500, F. W. Shelton. — *Democratic Review*, Vol. XIX. p. 123, J. W. Shelton.

ADDENDA.

Page 150, insert :

1796.

Title: POEMS ON THE DEATH OF PRISCILLA FARMER, by her grandson Charles Lloyd, Bristol : Printed by N. Biggs, and sold by James Phillips, George-yard. Lombard Street. 8vo pp.

Note. Lamb's poem " The Grandame " appears here for the first time. It was prefaced thus : " The following beautiful fragment was written by Charles Lamb of the India House. Its subject being the same with that of my poems, I was solicitous to have it printed with them, and I am indebted to a Friend of the author for the permission."

Page 155, insert :

1807.

Title: TIME'S A TELL-TALE : | A COMEDY, | In Five Acts, | as performed at the | Theatre-Royal, Drury-Lane, | [Quotation] by Henry Siddons. | London : | Printed for Longman, Hurst, Rees and Orme, | Pater-noster Row, | 1807. | 8vo

Collation : Title, 1 page, 1 blank page, Preface. 2 pages,
Prologue, 1 page, Dramatis Personæ, 1 page.   pp. 1-67,
1 blank page, Epilogue, 2 pages.   Size 8 x 5.
Note.   Charles Lamb wrote the Epilogue.

Page 162, insert :

1828.

Title : THE BIJOU ; | or | Annual of Literature | and
the arts. | London | William Pickering, | Chancery Lane. |
1828. | 18mo
Collation : Frontispiece, Engraved Title, Dedication, Preface,
and Contents.   pp. xiv. pp. 319.   Size 6½ x 4.
Note.   To this Annual Lamb contributed " Verses for an Album " and
the poem beginning " Fresh clad from heaven in robes of white."
      Price.   New York, 1892. $2.00.   Pickering & Chatto
(1892).   £1.15.

Page 168, insert before *Englishman's Magazine,* September,
      1831 :

August, 1831, " Hercules Pacificatus.   A tale from Suidas."
[Signed C. L.]

Page 168, insert before *The Gem,* 1830 :

Gem (*The*), 1829, [edited by Leigh Hunt], "On an infant
dying as soon as it was born," " In my own Album."

Page 176, insert before 1814 :

1811. Mrs. Leicester's School ; or. the History of Several
Young Ladies related by themselves.   First American edition.
Georgetown, 1811.   24mo.

Page 177, insert before 1835. Specimens of English Dramatic
      Poets :

1817. Specimens of English Dramatic Poets, who lived
about the time of Shakespeare.   Third edition, printed for
John Bumpus, 1817.   12mo.

Page 178, insert after 1854. Specimens of English Dramatic Poets :

1859. —— The Same. A new edition complete in one volume. New York, 1859. 12mo.

Page 179, insert after 1846. Tales from Shakespeare :

1853. Tales from Shakespeare for the use of young persons, by Charles and Mary Lamb [wood-cuts.] New York, 1852. 12mo.

Page 180, insert after 1888. Tales from Shakespeare:

1891. Tales from Shakespeare. Comedies and Tragedies. Edited with notes by W. T. Rolfe. Illustrated. New York, 1891. 2 vols. 16mo.